Re

Red Snow

LARRAINE S HARRISON

Acknowledgements

With thanks to all my family for their support and practical help with the editing and production of this book. Thanks also to my grand-daughters Esther and Ivy, who love stories. I hope they will enjoy reading this one.

1

The Stalker

Stalking the boy next door in the middle of the night was a dangerous thing for a twelve-year-old girl to do, but Megan just had to find out where he was going.

She looked at the bedroom clock. It was ten minutes to midnight; time to get ready. She tried to ignore the butterflies in her stomach. Whilst the thought of what she was about to do terrified her, it also excited her and took her mind off all her troubles.

She got out of bed, pulled her red curly hair into a ponytail and put on her warmest clothes for the cold winter night. Moving towards her bedroom window, she climbed up on to the broad window sill so she had a good view of the street outside. Then she waited.

A few minutes later, a dim light came on in the bedroom of the house next door. Thirteen-year-old Ryan got out of bed. He got dressed, put a torch and a phone in one of his jacket pockets, swung a bag on his back and turned out the bedside light. Creeping along the landing to his grandad Bill's bedroom, he peered inside. When he was satisfied that Bill's hearing aid was on the bedside table, he set off down the dark stairs, holding the handrail to guide him. Once in the kitchen, he switched on his torch. Bill's dog, Skippy, raised her sleek head and stared at him with her huge brown eyes.

'Stay there, Skippy,' Ryan whispered. 'It's OK.'

The old dog wagged her tail weakly and went back to sleep. Ryan reached in his pocket and pulled out his door key. Then he carefully unlocked the back door and moved swiftly out of the house.

As soon as Megan saw Ryan in the street, she sprang into action. She could hear her father snoring in the room next to hers as she moved with hurrying steps down the softly carpeted stairs. Once in the hallway, she stepped into her boots, took the spare key from a nearby shelf, put on her woolly hat and opened the front door. Seconds later, she was following Ryan down the street. He was some way ahead, so she knew she would have to run to catch him up. Megan was small for her age, but she was a good runner and within minutes she had closed the gap between them. Then she hung back. She needed to keep Ryan a safe distance away before slowing her pace to match his. Keeping her eyes on him all the time, Megan walked close to the houses. If he should look back, she would flatten herself against a garden wall or push into a hedge for cover.

It wasn't long before Ryan reached a point along Oakton Road, where there were no more houses and no more street lights. With only the moon to light her way, Megan now had to walk a little closer to Ryan, to keep him in sight. Although this increased the risk of her being seen, she was determined not to lose him. It was at this point that something crossed her mind. If Ryan continued along this road, he would eventually reach the entrance to Oakton Hall, with its security lights and CCTV cameras. If he were to pass this entrance, she would have to abandon the stalking. There was no way she could risk being caught on camera. But before Ryan reached the security lights, he turned off the road onto a footpath into Oakton woods.

Megan used to visit these woods with her mother, when she was a young child, but she hadn't been there for many years. A network of circular tracks snaked up and down the steeply wooded slopes, but she knew that if Ryan kept to the footpath, he would eventually come out onto the main road to York.

She hesitated for a moment. The woods were dark and forbidding. She was afraid of the dark, but to walk back alone on an unlit road was probably just as scary. With this in mind, she took a deep breath and followed Ryan into the woods.

Along the right-hand side of the moonlit footpath, part of an ancient stone wall cast a shadow over the path, making it difficult for Megan to see. On the other side of the path, the dense, dark pine trees sloped upwards, sending strange whispering noises into the midnight air. The beam of Ryan's torch told her that he was still walking the path ahead, but the overarching shadows of the trees meant that Megan could no longer see him properly. Afraid to use the small torch in her coat pocket, in case it attracted Ryan's attention, she stumbled along the path, following the beams of Ryan's torch. But the path was winding and when Ryan rounded the bends, the torchlight disappeared altogether, leaving Megan following blindly until the light reappeared.

After some time, Ryan stopped in a clearing, where the footpath forked. Megan remembered that the right-hand fork led to a woodyard and two gatehouses. There was a bench at the fork, made from an old log. From where she was standing, Megan had a good view of Ryan as he sat uneasily on the bench, but if he were to shine his torch back along the main path, she would be seen. Thinking quickly, she stepped off the path into the damp, soggy undergrowth. Even though she was some distance away, she could see that Ryan had placed his torch on the bench and was now unpacking his bag. She thought that if she headed far enough back into the trees, she could make her way round towards the bench, so she would end up just behind it. From this position, she could watch Ryan without being seen.

Threads of moonlight filtered down through the webbed

branches making it just possible for Megan to see her way through the trees, but it wasn't easy. The tangled brambles that twined the woodland floor, scratched mercilessly at her legs as she crept softly through the undergrowth, like a cat stalking its prey. When she finally reached the trees some way behind the bench, she noticed a narrow track leading up the slope. Stepping over the track, she positioned herself behind a large tree.

Ryan had his back to Megan, but she could see that he had placed a number of things beside him on the bench. She could see something that looked like a water bottle, but to her annoyance she couldn't make out what the other things were. She couldn't see what he was doing either, but whatever it was, it seemed to be taking a long time.

There was nothing else she could do except stand and wait. She pulled her hat down over her ears. The night was growing colder.

Several minutes later, Ryan began to put things back into his bag. Megan braced herself ready to follow him, but this was a move she was never to make, because in the next few seconds, the stalking would be over.

As Ryan placed the last few items in his bag, something terrifying happened. A high-pitched screech rang through the woods, tearing into the silence – a deeply lonely sound, ringing through the woods, like the cry of a tormented animal. Megan watched helplessly as Ryan grabbed his bag and ran as fast as he could back along the path until he disappeared from view.

Then there was silence; a strange, eerie silence, broken only by the scuffling of some small animal as it hastened through the undergrowth. Megan stood motionless. Her mind was reeling. She could see nothing out there, so which way was she to run?

Then a second cry arose, similar to the first, piercing through the night with a haunting shrillness. It echoed around the woods so strangely that it was difficult to know exactly where it was coming from. Megan took the small torch from her pocket. Frantically circling the beams, she illuminated the trees one after another, searching for some clue as to what had made such a chilling sound.

It was then that she saw it. A dark shape, moving in the distance. A large four-legged creature, curling its way around the trees. Standing as big as a very large dog, it had the head of a huge cat and a long bushy tail. Silently, softly, weaving its way around the trees, the cat-like creature was moving ever closer to where Megan was standing. She switched off her torch, but she could still see its fearful outline, moving slowly towards her. She had no time to lose. A creature like that with a keen sense of smell would soon know she was there. She cursed herself for being so stupid. Why had she put on a white coat? If she tried to run, it would attract the cat's attention. The only thing to do was to hide, in the desperate hope that the cat would wander off.

Slowly and carefully, she inched herself round towards the back of the tree, holding on to the bark with her small gloved hands. Shuffling her feet, one small step at a time, she kept her eyes constantly on the prowling cat. She was about halfway round the tree when the cat made a sudden stop and looked towards her. As it sniffed the air, she caught a glimpse of its piercing eyes, glowing golden in the moonlight. She stood very still and held her breath. Could it smell her fear?

Seconds later she heard a sound coming from the direction of the woodyard. It was a woman's voice calling out in a shrill tone: 'Miaow Miaow Here! Miaow!'

As the woman's torch came into view, Megan ran blindly towards her shouting:

'There's a big creature! A huge cat or something. It's over there!'

She turned to point back to where she had seen the creature, but in her panic, she stumbled over a fallen log. In reaching out to save herself, one of Megan's hands landed on something sharp. She winced as the pain shot through her wrist. Her blood felt strangely warm as it seeped through her woollen glove, onto the cuff of her white coat. Within seconds she felt an arm around her.

'It's alright!' said the woman, helping her up. 'It's OK.'

At that moment, they both looked up, just in time to see the creature slowly turn its long body and creep away, back into the darkness. Then it was gone.

The woman helped Megan towards the path. As she reached down to pick up the large bag she had dropped on the ground, Megan caught sight of the woman's hair. It was silvery grey and it hung down her back in a long plait.

'Come with me,' said the woman. 'We'll soon have you cleaned up.'

Megan eyed her warily. She would never have gone with this strange woman if she hadn't recognised her. The woman had once come to Megan's school to talk about the badgers in the woods. Megan couldn't remember her last name, but she knew she was called Irene and she lived in one of the gatehouses. By now Megan's hand was hurting badly. She just wanted to go home, but she was afraid to go back along the path after seeing the big cat. So, saying very little except to whisper 'Thank you,' Megan followed Irene back to the footpath.

'What are you doing out here alone at this time of night?' asked Irene sharply.

'Have you run away from home or something?'

Megan was shocked at the suggestion. 'No! I was just following someone.'

It was easier to see by the light of Irene's large torch and so they quickly reached the point where the footpath widened out into a narrow road. Not far along this road was a woodyard, with huge piles of cut logs and large up-ended tree trunks. As they rounded a slight bend in the road, a tall stone arch came into view, with a gatehouse on either side. These gatehouses were once cottages, guarding the old entrance to Oakton Hall, but they had now been converted into modern houses, with their own gardens. Megan noticed the large skip in the garden of the gatehouse on the left-hand side of the arch. It was piled high with builders' rubbish.

'Come on,' said Irene, steering Megan towards the gatehouse on the right. 'This way.'

Although this gatehouse was fairly small, it had a large garden to the side and back, surrounded by a high hedge. Megan wondered if the black car parked outside the house was Irene's, but she had no more time to think, because Irene was already opening the front door.

'You can leave your boots in here,' said Irene, dropping her large heavy bag onto the hallway floor. Megan obediently took off her boots. She decided to keep her coat and hat on, just in case she needed to leave in a hurry. She followed Irene into a large kitchen, where she peeled off her blood-stained glove and washed her wounded hand.

'You look frozen,' said Irene, handing Megan a large plaster. 'Put this on your hand and then go in there. I'll put the fire on.' She pointed to a small sitting room leading from the kitchen. Megan really wanted to go home, but as Irene had been kind enough to help her, she didn't feel she could refuse.

As she entered the room, Megan couldn't help but notice the many ornaments, books, and framed photographs, all untidily displayed on tables and shelves. A large black and white photo of a man standing by an old sports car hung on the wall above the fireplace. His face looked familiar, but she couldn't think who it was.

'Sit here and get warm,' said Irene gently as she lit the fire. 'I'll get you a hot drink.'

It was when she was left alone that Megan began to tremble. She began to realise what danger she had been in. If the big cat had attacked her, she could have been badly injured or even killed. She glanced at a clock on the wall. It was nearly two o'clock in the morning. She began to relax a little. The cat hadn't harmed her and there was plenty of time to have a drink and get back home before her dad woke up.

Warming herself by the fire made her feel a little better and after a while she began to take a closer look at Irene's room. There was something strangely familiar about it. She glanced at the shelf beside her chair, where a collection of cat ornaments were arranged in a line. There were several large china cats, a couple of smaller brass ones and a tiny wooden cat with sparkling eyes. But most unusual of all, right at the end of the shelf was a small wicker basket containing three white hand-knitted cats. Megan thought she might have played with a basket like this when she was a small child. As she looked at the cats her eyes were drawn to a small photo in a silver frame on the shelf above. She stood up, intending to take a closer look.

'I see you've found my cat collection,' said Irene, as she passed Megan a mug of tea.

Megan sat back down and cupped her cold hands around the warm mug. She watched as Irene sank into a big leather armchair on the opposite side of the room. Her weather-beaten face looked tired and wrinkled, but her blue eyes were bright and sharp.

She spoke in a soft voice. 'What's your name?'

'Megan.'

'I'm Irene. How old are you Megan? Ten or eleven?'

'I'm twelve,' said Megan indignantly.

'That's far too young to be wandering alone in the woods,

in the middle of the night?' said Irene. 'What were you doing?'

'I was following a boy called Ryan,' explained Megan. 'He's come to live next door with his grandad, while his parents finish doing up a house in the next village.'

'And how old is Ryan?' asked Irene.

'I think he's thirteen.'

Irene's eyes widened. 'That's also too young to be going out alone at night. Where was he going?'

'I don't know,' replied Megan. 'That's why I followed him.' She paused to sip her drink.

'You need to tell me a bit more than that,' said Irene.

'It started one night last week, just after midnight,' said Megan. 'I heard next door's gate creak and when I looked out of my bedroom window, I saw Ryan setting off down the road, with a bag on his back.'

'Are you often awake at midnight?' asked Irene.

Megan nodded. 'I don't sleep very well.'

'How long was Ryan gone?' asked Irene.

'I went back to bed before he came back,' said Megan, 'but the next night I stayed awake and he was gone at least an hour.'

Irene shook her head in disbelief. 'You mean he makes a habit of going out at that time of night?'

'Yes,' said Megan. 'He's been out every night this week.'

Irene looked astounded. 'So, you just decided to follow him, did you? Didn't it occur to you that you might be putting yourself in danger?'

'I thought I would be safe, if I made sure Ryan was in front of me all the time,' said Megan.

Irene sighed. 'Well I just hope your parents don't wake up and find you missing, or you'll have the police to answer to.'

Megan was beginning to feel uncomfortable. The blazing fire was making the small cluttered room hot and stuffy. She pulled off her hat and stuffed it into her coat pocket.

'There's only my dad,' she said. 'My mum died a few years ago. You won't tell my dad, will you? If you walk back with me now, I can get home before he wakes up. He's only got me you see and he's not been well and…'

Without warning, Irene lurched forward in her chair, staring strangely at Megan's face.

'What's your last name Megan?'

'It's Townsend,' she replied 'Why?'

Irene's expression changed. Her lined face furrowed into a scowl. There was panic in her eyes.

'I need to walk you home now,' she said abruptly. 'If anyone finds out you've been here, I could get into trouble.'

Rising from her chair, she marched briskly back into the kitchen. Megan followed her. 'What kind of trouble?' Megan asked.

Irene seemed flustered as she passed Megan her boots. 'People could say I kidnapped you or something. You must never tell anyone you've been here.'

Megan put on her boots in silence. She was shocked at how Irene had changed and she couldn't understand why.

Neither of them spoke as they set off back towards the woodyard, but after several minutes Megan broke the silence. 'What if the big cat sees us?' she asked.

Irene stopped and turned towards her sharply. 'There is no big cat. It was probably a large domestic cat you saw, or a fox or something.'

Megan was exasperated. 'But I saw it,' she protested. 'We both saw it. It was looking at us when I fell. It came through the woods after that screeching sound. You must have heard that sound. You must have seen it.'

Irene set off again with ever quickening steps. 'There are all sorts of animals in these woods Megan,' she said, 'and they make all sorts of sounds.'

Megan was defiant. 'It was definitely a big cat,' she murmured.

Irene raised her voice. 'I'm telling you, there is no big cat. I've lived here for many years and believe me, if there was a big cat, I would've seen it.'

Keeping up with Irene wasn't easy, but Megan still had another question to ask her. 'Were you looking for a lost pet in the woods?' she asked breathlessly.

'What do you mean?' said Irene, slowing down a little.

'I heard you calling for something just before you found me,' said Megan. There was an awkward pause, before Irene replied. 'I was just out for a walk. I couldn't sleep. It was probably an animal you heard.'

Megan felt angry. It was obvious that Irene was lying.

When they reached the wooden bench, where the path forked, Megan quickly shone her torch around it. She wanted to see if Ryan had left anything behind, but there was nothing there. They hurried on in silence, until they finally reached the end of the woodland path and turned into the road, but before they reached the start of the houses, Irene came to a sudden stop. She turned to face Megan. 'Listen,' she said firmly. 'Don't ever tell anyone you have been to see me, or I will get into trouble. And don't scare people by telling them there's a big cat in the woods either. Do you understand? This is important.'

Megan nodded. Irene managed a weak smile. 'I will have to leave you here Megan, but you're almost home. I'll watch you until you get to the street lights.'

Megan tried to smile back, but she just couldn't make herself do it. Irene had lied to her and she was still feeling angry. 'Thank you for helping me,' was all she could bring herself to say.

'Look after your dad,' muttered Irene. 'And take care of yourself.'

It was not yet dawn as Megan ran to the start of the houses on Oakton Road, where the street lights were still on. Then she turned and looked back. Irene was still standing by the roadside. It was when she reached her garden gate that she began to feel uneasy. She wondered how Irene knew she lived on Oakton Road. She was sure she didn't tell her. She was beginning to think that Irene knew more about her than she was letting on.

Megan glanced up at Ryan's bedroom. There was a light on, so at least he had got home safely. She turned the key in the door and slipped back into her house as silently as she had left. Once the spare key was safely back on the shelf, she quickly bundled her blood-stained coat and gloves into the washing machine. She pushed them right to the back of the drum and then carefully covered them with a towel to hide the blood. Then she crept upstairs, got undressed and climbed into bed, as if nothing had happened.

2

Red Snow

The next morning was the first day of the school half-term holiday and there was a light dusting of snow on the ground. At 9.30 a.m. Ryan's grandad Bill set off to a coffee morning at the community centre. Ryan was just getting up when he heard someone knocking. When he eventually opened the door, he was surprised to see that it was Megan.

'Bill's out,' he mumbled sleepily. 'He won't be back 'til lunchtime.'

'I know,' she answered. 'It's you I want to see. Can I come in?'

Megan had been thinking all night about what she was going to say to Ryan. She wasn't very good at talking to boys. She usually tried to avoid them at school, but this was an exception. She had to warn Ryan about the big cat and there was no easy way of putting it. Bill would be back in an hour or so. She would just have to tell Ryan the truth about what she saw and she would have to tell it quickly.

'I know it was stupid, but I followed you last night,' she blurted out. 'I don't know what you were doing in the woods Ryan, but it's too dangerous. There's a big cat on the loose. I was lucky to escape. It was looking straight at me.'

There was a stunned look on Ryan's face as he paused for a moment to take in what Megan had just said. Then he became angry. 'You've got no right to be following me!' he shouted.

'I couldn't sleep, so I went for a walk that's all. There's no law against going for a walk at night is there?'

Megan interrupted him sharply. 'Don't pretend this was a one-off thing Ryan, because it wasn't. I've seen you leaving the house every night for the last few nights. If you don't tell me what's going on, I'll tell Bill.'

Ryan's face reddened with rage. 'Oh no you won't,' he snapped, 'because if you do, your dad will know you've been out alone at night. And he won't be very pleased to hear that, will he?'

'Well I wasn't alone, was I?' she retorted. 'You were just in front of me until you ran off.'

Ryan raised his voice in frustration. 'Well I didn't know you were there, did I? How can you blame me for running off and leaving you when I didn't even know you were there?'

Megan was usually a calm person, but Ryan's attitude was beginning to annoy her. All she was doing was trying to warn him.

'I'm not blaming you,' she said curtly. 'All I said was that I didn't go out alone, because you were always in my sight.'

There was a brief pause as their eyes momentarily drifted towards the window, where thick snowflakes were gliding softly onto the road outside.

'If you followed me you must have heard what I heard,' said Ryan.

Megan sat down on one of Bill's comfy chairs. At last she felt she was getting somewhere. 'I did hear it,' she said. 'It was a horrible screeching sound. I think it might have been an animal.'

Ryan sat down on the settee and gazed absentmindedly at the fireplace.

Speaking more softly than before, Megan tried again.

'What were you doing in the woods Ryan?'

He looked at Megan. His face was tired and drawn. 'You

have to promise not to tell anyone. Not Bill, not your dad, not anyone.'

Megan nodded. 'I promise.'

'Last weekend, after we'd had all that snow,' he said, 'I took Skippy to Oakton woods. She goes mad when it's been snowing. She runs about like a puppy, kicking up all the snow ...

Megan was becoming impatient. 'What happened? Did you see something?'

'Red snow,' said Ryan.

Megan sat upright. 'What?'

Ryan lowered his voice. 'Bloodstains on the snow,' he said.

Skippy barked as a key turned in the door.

'I'm back,' called Bill from the hallway. 'The heating's broken at the community centre.'

Before Ryan and Megan had time to think, Bill was walking into the lounge. 'Oh, hello Megan. Have you come to visit our Ryan?' Bill winked mischievously at Megan. 'He needs a girlfriend to go out with, don't you Ryan?'

Ryan's face flushed with embarrassment. 'I'm OK Grandad,' he protested.

But Bill was persistent. 'Megan goes to a swimming club at that new leisure centre at Oakton Hall. Why don't you get down there and join something, instead of idling around here all day?'

'I take Skippy out all the time,' said Ryan indignantly.

'Yes, and half the time she doesn't want to go,' laughed Bill. 'Dragging her out in all weathers. She's an old dog like me. She must be the most exhausted Lurcher in Yorkshire.'

Ryan gave Megan a knowing look. Bill had given him an idea. 'That's why Megan's here Grandad. She wants to show me round the leisure centre today. She's just going to ask her dad if it's OK.'

This was news to Megan, but she went along with it all the same. Ryan's strange comment about the blood on the snow had unnerved her and she needed somewhere private where she could talk to him. The leisure centre seemed as good a place as any. She was just hoping her dad would let her go.

'Why go today?' murmured Bill. 'It's started snowing again.'

'It's not like you to be put off by a bit of snow Grandad,' said Ryan.

Bill groaned as he reached for his newspaper. He was a large, jolly man who had always been active. He was a gifted mechanic and still had a keen interest in fixing cars, but now he was retired he was spending more time in his chair than in his garage. 'Suit yourself,' he replied, waving his folded newspaper in the air. 'Oh, to be young again. I used to love the snow. We used to go sledging on a tin tray. We used to sneak into Oakton Hall grounds and then sledge down that slope to the lake. I remember once when we nearly got caught …'

Bill was always interesting to listen to. He told such funny stories of when he was young. Megan used to love coming to see him with her mum when she was small. But he tended to talk for rather a long time once he got started and today she needed time to speak to Ryan alone.

'We've got to go now Uncle Bill,' she said gently. 'We want to get to the Hall this morning in case it shuts early and I have to ask my dad if I can go.'

Bill turned towards Megan with a more serious look. 'How is your dad by the way? Haven't seen him for a while.'

Megan turned her eyes to the floor. She hated it when people asked her about her dad. The only way to stop them asking awkward questions was to tell them he was fine. 'He's not too bad,' she murmured.

'Maybe I'll look in on him some time soon.' said Bill kindly.

Megan smiled weakly but said nothing.

'Well go on then if you're going!' shouted Bill, waving them away. 'Have a good time.'

'Tell your dad we may be gone for a while,' said Ryan as he opened the door for Megan to leave.

'Er… My dad's not usually keen on letting me go places without him,' she said awkwardly. 'But he may let me go if you're there when I ask him.'

Ryan shrugged his shoulders. 'OK,' he said. 'I'll just tell Grandad I'm going with you.'

Paul Townsend was sitting in his untidy lounge finishing a mug of tea, when Megan arrived with Ryan. Peering awkwardly into the darkly curtained room, Ryan could just make out the figure of Megan's dad slumped in an armchair. He had heard his grandad mention Megan's dad, Paul, but this was the first time they had met.

Megan seemed on edge as she moved some newspapers off the settee and invited Ryan to sit down beside her. Despite the darkness in the room, Ryan could see that, although Paul was fully dressed, he looked disheveled and unshaven, as if he had just got out of bed.

'This is Ryan,' said Megan, 'Bill's grandson.' Paul nodded but remained silent.

Ryan sat uncomfortably on the edge of the settee as Megan chatted nervously about the snow and about how Bill's coffee morning had been cancelled, but Paul just stared vacantly at the floor as if he wasn't really listening.

'Uncle Bill wants me to show Ryan round the leisure centre this morning,' said Megan hesitantly.

Paul raised his head and looked across to Megan. 'What have you done to your hand?'

Megan jumped. She pulled the sleeve of her jumper over the plaster on her hand. 'Oh, it's nothing. … er … I … tripped over yesterday,' she stammered.

Paul's eyes flashed. 'Why can't you be more careful?'

'Sorry,' whispered Megan meekly.

Paul sighed and returned his gaze to the floor.

'Will it be OK if I go to the leisure centre, Dad?' asked Megan. 'I'll stay with Ryan all the time.'

There was an awkward silence as Paul thought for quite a while before replying.

When he finally did, his voice was slow and grave. 'I suppose it will be alright. But make sure you look after her Ryan. She's all I've got.'

Now it was Megan's turn to feel embarrassed, but Ryan just nodded reassuringly.

'We may be gone for a while Dad,' said Megan cheerily, as she moved towards the window. 'I'd like to show Ryan the new swimming pool and all the sports facilities and we may go to the café.'

As she opened the curtains, Megan glanced down the street. 'There's a police car outside Mrs Harris' bungalow,' she said.

Paul rose laboriously from his chair and wandered across to the window. 'Not another burglary,' he sighed.

Ryan joined them to take a look for himself. 'My grandad's friend Mary was burgled last week,' said Ryan. 'They took all her rings and even her family's war medals.'

Paul slowly returned to his chair. 'These criminals don't care about anyone but themselves,' he said bitterly. 'This village is full of scum, Ryan. Do you know that? They'll rob you of your last penny if they get the chance. What a terrible world we live in.'

Megan was used to her dad having these dark thoughts, but she felt embarrassed when other people had to listen to them. 'Bill said he might call in to see you some time,' she said, trying to lighten the mood.

Paul grunted in reply, but as Megan moved towards his chair to pick up the empty mug on his table, he banged his clenched fist violently onto the arm of his chair, knocking the mug onto the floor. 'Why can't you just leave things alone?' he yelled. 'I was still drinking that. Now look what you've made me do!'

There was an uneasy silence as Megan gently put the mug back on the table and then went to get a cloth to wipe up the dregs of tea spattered on the carpet. When she returned, she spoke to her dad without looking at him, wiping the carpet as if nothing had happened. 'I switched the washing machine on earlier,' she said. 'I'll empty it when I get back.'

Paul made no move, but his voice was now more subdued. 'I can surely manage to sort out a washing machine myself,' he muttered. 'I'm not totally helpless. And anyway, what are you washing now? I never get any peace from the sound of that washing machine.'

Ryan was uneasy. He just wanted to leave. 'Shall I get my coat then Megan?' he said.

Paul let out another sigh before turning to face Ryan. 'Just a minute. Did you say you were going to the café?' he asked.

'Only if we have time,' said Ryan nervously.

Paul stood up and reached into his trouser pocket. 'Here,' he said, handing Megan some cash, 'get yourselves something in the café, but be careful in this snow. I don't want to end up taking you to hospital if you fall. I've got enough to worry about as it is.'

When Ryan finally left to get his coat, Megan went to the kitchen to check her list of jobs on the wall. She had already turned on the washing machine and washed the dishes, but all the other jobs like the ironing and the cleaning would have to wait. She was thankful it was half-term – she would have time to do them later in the week.

Paul came out of the lounge as Megan went into the hallway to get her coat. He watched her as she reached for the waterproof jacket that she wore to school. 'It's too cold for that thin thing today!' he snapped. 'Where's your white padded coat?'

'I told you ages ago Dad; it doesn't fit me properly anymore.'

'I find that hard to believe Megan. I only bought it last year. Where is it?'

Megan zipped up her jacket and fished in the pockets for her other gloves. 'It's in the washing machine. I got mud on it when I tripped over,' she said quickly.

Paul frowned 'I'll have to get you another one in a bigger size.'

'No Dad! I don't like that style anymore.'

Megan was frustrated. Her dad was stuck in a time warp. How she hated wearing the same kind of clothes she had worn when she was a little girl. But this was not the time to start an argument with her father. She knew from past experience that if something upset him he could so easily change his mind about letting her go out.

'See you later Dad,' she said quickly, as she closed the door swiftly behind her, before he had chance to call her back.

Ryan was standing in the street waiting for her. He was carrying the same backpack that he'd taken to the woods the night before.

'What have you got in there?' asked Megan. 'It looks heavy.'

'It'll all make sense when we get to the woods,' said Ryan as they set off along the road.

Megan was surprised. 'What do you mean? I thought we were going to the leisure centre at the Hall, not the woods.'

By now Ryan was almost running. 'We are going to the Hall, but I need to go to the woods first.'

Megan pulled at Ryan's sleeve. 'I'm not going anywhere unless you tell me what this is all about,' she said. 'What did you mean when you said there were bloodstains on the snow?'

Ryan shook her off. 'I'm going to show you if you'll just let me,' he said. 'Then you'll know why I need to hurry. Just follow me. We need to be quick if we're going to the Hall as well.'

Although Megan was curious, she was also scared of what Ryan might be leading her into. When they reached the footpath that led to the woods, she hesitated. 'What about the cat?' she said.

Ryan picked up a large fallen branch by the path and offered it to Megan. 'Take this if you're worried, but big cats don't usually hunt during the daytime. Anyway, there are other people around today. We'll be OK,' he said reassuringly.

Megan wasn't convinced that a stick would be any use against a big cat, but she took it just the same and the two of them set off, walking briskly. The snow had stopped now and the winter sun was struggling to shine. Its faint warmth was comforting as it filtered through the branches, lighting up the snow-smothered land.

Two youths wearing hoodies passed by as they started along the path, but they met no-one else until they came to the bench where the path forked. It was there that they saw a woman running down the small track towards the bench. The woman looked anxious as she slithered and slipped down the steep track, but when she saw Megan and Ryan she put on a broad fixed grin. She looked striking, dressed in white running gear, with a white hat pulled over her black curly hair. She had a large bag on her back.

'Hi Megan,' she gasped. 'Can't stop. I'm training for the York marathon. Are you coming to swimming club next week? The new pool's open now. It's fantastic.'

'I think so,' replied Megan. 'This is Ryan. He might be joining the club after half-term.'

'Oh great. See you both there then,' she called, as she joined the main path and headed towards Oakton Road.

'Who's that?' asked Ryan suspiciously.

'It's Kirsty. She's one of the swimming teachers at the Hall. Why? What's the problem?'

Ryan shrugged his shoulders. 'I've seen her a lot when I've been walking the dog that's all. She's always grinning and waving to people and she's always got that huge bag on her back.'

Ryan was jumpy. Having first looked around to reassure himself there were no more passers-by, he set off up the steep track behind the bench, with Megan close behind.

They followed the narrow track as it wound its way around the trees, until they came across a wooden signpost. Carved on the post were the words: *To the WATCHTOWER.*

Ryan set off in the direction of the arrow. 'Not far now,' he announced.

Megan followed warily, her eyes ever watchful for the big cat. It was not until they reached the highest part of the woods, where the land flattened out, that Ryan came to a stop. 'Be very quiet now,' he whispered. 'We're heading over there.'

Megan followed his gaze. In the distance was a small cylindrical stone tower that had become darkened and brown with age. It was standing alone in the centre of a cleared patch of ground. 'What is it?' asked Megan.

Ryan stooped down to pick up a red cigarette packet that someone had carelessly thrown away. He stuffed it angrily into his pocket before he replied. 'It's a disused watchtower,' he said confidently. 'It was built years ago by the Squire of Oakton Hall, so he could watch the wildlife.'

Megan stared at the distant tower. 'You mean a sort of bird hide?' she asked.

'Sort of,' said Ryan.

'It was about here that I first saw it,' he added.

'Saw what?' asked Megan.

'The red snow,' said Ryan. 'There was a trail of blood leading to the tower.'

Megan was becoming alarmed. 'Whose blood was it?'

But Ryan didn't answer. 'This way,' he whispered as he set off towards the tower.

'When we get there Megan, keep near me and don't make any sudden noises.'

Although she was intrigued, Megan asked no more questions. She followed Ryan as he crept slowly across the cleared grassy area until they came to a point where they could see the arched entrance to the tower. Then Megan drew back. She could hear a strange low growling sound. It seemed to be coming from inside the tower itself.

'Come on,' said Ryan. 'Keep with me.'

As they moved closer to the tower, Megan could see that the entrance was protected by a wrought-iron gate, fastened securely with a heavy padlock. The locked gate meant that it was impossible for a person to enter the tower, but the gap under the gate was big enough for an animal to squeeze through.

Ryan pointed to the gate. 'There's a cat inside there,' he said quietly.

It only took one glance through the bars of the gate to convince Megan that this was no ordinary cat. Staring back at her from within the tower were the same wild golden eyes she had seen the night before, only this time the cat was slightly smaller. She noticed that it had an unusual marking on its forehead that looked vaguely like a letter M and it had dark lines running from its eyes to its ears. With its snarling mouth wide open, its rasping red tongue revealed a row of sharp sabre-like teeth as it hissed and spat in wild fury. Ryan took a small step closer to the bars of the gate. Then POW! It banged one of its huge forepaws loudly down onto the ground and lashed out with its other paw, revealing its long, sharp claws.

Ryan sprang back. 'It did that when I first found it,' he said.

'It scared Skippy so much that she ran off. It took me ages to find her.'

He looked again into the tower. 'The blood on the snow was from its injured leg,' he said. 'It must have dragged itself into the tower, but now I think it's too weak to come out. It needs a chance to recover. It'll die if I don't keep feeding it.'

Megan was shaken by the ferocity of what she had seen. She spoke in a hushed voice.

'What kind of cat *is* it?'

Ryan began to unpack his bag. He took out a water bottle, a small carton of milk, a pack of sausages, a plastic bowl and something wrapped in a tea towel. 'I don't really know,' he replied, 'but I looked it up on the internet and I think it might be something called a wild cat.' He poured some of the milk into the bowl and added some water. 'They're an endangered species,' he continued 'and they're very fierce. They could rip your arm to shreds with those claws. That's why I bring these.' He pulled out two pairs of Bill's long leather gardening gloves from his bag and laid them on the ground.

'Is this what you've been doing every night?' asked Megan.

'Grandad would want to know where I was going if I went out in the daytime without Skippy,' said Ryan, 'and he would want to know what I was carrying in this bag as well. I only managed to sneak the bag out today because he was reading the paper.'

Megan was still puzzled. 'Why don't you just tell Uncle Bill you've found a cat? He loves animals.'

Ryan sighed. 'Megan this is not an ordinary cat. If people find out there are big cats here, they'll be hunted. It's an endangered species and it's got to be kept secret. No-one must find out.'

'But Ryan, they're dangerous. You shouldn't …' But her words were cut short when she saw Ryan taking a small knife from inside the tea towel.

'Don't worry. It's only an old kitchen knife,' said Ryan. 'I use it to cut the sausages into small pieces on the bench, so when I get up here, all I have to do is put on the gloves and throw the pieces of sausage through the bars into the tower. I couldn't cut them up on the bench today, because someone might see me.' He could see by Megan's face that she still didn't understand. 'It's a wild animal,' he said. 'It gets stressed when people are nearby, so I try to be as quick as I can when I'm here.'

Ryan seemed to know what he was doing, but the sound of the cat's low menacing growl in the background was making Megan feel nervous.

'I'm trying a new bowl,' said Ryan, standing up. 'The saucer I've been using doesn't hold much liquid, so I needed something bigger.'

Megan could hear the growling getting louder and louder, as Ryan moved back towards the tower, carrying the gloves and the bowl of milk. She thought it sounded like a lion. It was the fiercest thing she had ever seen.

Megan watched anxiously as Ryan put on both pairs of gloves and slowly, very slowly, slid the bowl under the iron gate, towards the growling cat. There was a brief silence before it pounced. Its long horn-coloured talons shot through the bars towards Ryan's gloved hand, tearing into the leather with a sickening scraping sound. It then fell back as if exhausted and bit the rim of the bowl with its sabre-like teeth, spilling most of the milk onto its body as it did so. Ryan gave a shout and leapt back to safety, pulling off the gloves to examine his hand. There were red marks on his skin, but luckily the claws hadn't cut deep enough to draw blood. He sighed heavily and shook his head. 'I should have known it would tip the bowl.'

Megan waited a moment before she dared to creep close enough to peer into the tower once more. 'Look Ryan,' she said softly. 'It's licking the milk.'

Standing at a safe distance, both of them watched as the cat licked the milk from its body and then lapped up the little drops of milk left in the bowl.

'It must be starving,' said Megan 'Where are the sausages?'

'Be careful,' warned Ryan passing her the packet. 'It attacks the food as soon as it sees it.' He threw her the gloves. 'Better put these on just in case.'

Megan looked at them 'They're too big for me,' she said. 'Don't worry. I've got a good aim. I'll throw the sausages in from a safe distance.'

'Let me do it,' offered Ryan.

Megan shook her head. 'No. I want to try.'

There was something about this savage creature that Megan admired. It saddened her to think that something so wild and free wasn't strong enough to get out and feed itself.

Tearing open the pack of sausages, she took the knife and carefully cut the sausages into small pieces before carrying them towards the tower.

'Don't throw them all in,' warned Ryan. 'You never know when we might need some meat!'

'What do you mean?' asked Megan.

'We might meet the cat you saw last night,' said Ryan.

His words sent a shiver down Megan's spine. If this cat was fierce, then the bigger cat was likely to be even fiercer.

She could hear the cat in the tower hissing and spitting as she drew near. Taking a deep breath, she threw most of the sausages in through the bars of the gate as quickly as she could. Ryan was right, the cat fell on the food in a flash, devouring it instantly with a loud whirring growl. Megan stood back and waited until the cat had finished, before venturing forward to take another look. As she stared into the tower, her eyes became adjusted to the dimness. The cat had now backed up against the far wall of the tower and was crouched underneath what looked like a small wooden seat. It was sitting on something that resembled an old sack, but Megan could see something else. 'Ryan,' she called urgently. 'Come and look at this.'

On closer inspection, they could see that the sacking was actually a bag of some kind. It looked like the cat had clawed at it to make some bedding. Ryan went to get his torch and shone it into the tower. The cat began to hiss and spit again as the light shone onto its face. But there was no mistaking it. There was something in the bag. They could see a piece of material peeping out, but there was something larger and more solid underneath.

'There's no way we can get the bag out with the cat still in there,' declared Ryan, 'and anyway it's probably too far away for us to reach it through the bars.'

Megan was puzzled. 'How did it get in there? The gate has a lock on it.' She pulled at the gate to test it and the cat lunged forward again with its huge paws, hissing and spitting with fury. They both leapt back in alarm. The golden eyes of the cat, with their deep fathomless black pupils, were now fixed on them with a steely stare.

'I'll have to leave the bowl with the cat,' said Ryan trying to be more light-hearted. 'There's no way I'm going to reach into that tower again in a hurry.' He laughed nervously, but Megan didn't respond. She was looking back into the tower. She was still feeling sorry for the cat. Although technically it could get out of the tower, it was too weak and sick to break out of its prison.

'The cat I saw last night was much bigger than this one,' said Megan eventually.

Ryan looked worried. 'How big?'

'At least as big as a small panther,' she replied.

'Perhaps the one you saw is the bigger male cat and the one in the tower is a female,' suggested Ryan.

As they walked back down the path, Megan tried to find

out what Ryan knew about wild cats, but it turned out he didn't know very much.

'They're usually found in the Highlands of Scotland,' he said, 'They're much bigger and fiercer than domestic cats.'

'How did they get *here*?' she asked. 'Yorkshire's a long way from Scotland.'

'Someone must have brought them here,' he said thoughtfully. 'But the question is… who, and why?' He paused. 'And I'll tell you what else I'm wondering about,' he added. 'I'm wondering what's in that bag and I'm wondering when and how it got there.'

3

Storm

Once they reached the bench, Megan expected to walk back the way they had come, so she was surprised when Ryan set off in the opposite direction towards the woodyard.

'We need to take the short cut to the Hall,' he declared. 'It'll take too long to go back the way we came. Come on.'

Megan called after him. 'I think that way comes out on the York Road. That's not a short cut.'

'I know another way,' he called back. 'I've been before with Skippy. There's a footpath at the side of one of those gatehouses near the woodyard. It leads straight to the Hall.'

Megan was reluctant to follow him. She didn't really want to meet Irene again, but with the threat of a wild cat on the loose, she wasn't about to leave Ryan's side, no matter where he was going.

A strong wind was now blowing through the woods, bending the tall pine trees with violent gusts. Megan pulled up the hood of her jacket and began to wish she was wearing her white padded coat.

It wasn't long before they reached the woodyard. The snow on the ground had almost melted now, but there were still traces of snow on the piles of logs. Ryan glanced at one of the large logs as they hurried past the entrance to the yard, but then made a sudden stop.

'What is it?' she asked.

'Tracks,' said Ryan, pointing to the log. 'Look. Those are from a very large animal. Look at the size of those paws and look how far apart they are.'

Megan stared incredulously at the large paw marks in the snow. She felt a fear rising in the pit of her stomach. 'It's the big cat,' she said. 'It's been in the woodyard.'

Ryan reached out and gently touched her arm. 'Let's go,' he said softly.

Keeping on high alert, they finally approached the stone archway that linked the two gatehouses. Megan was relieved to see there was no car outside. There was no garage, so she felt she could safely assume that Irene was out. However, as they walked past the high hedges of Irene's garden, Megan had an uneasy feeling. It was the same feeling she had experienced in Irene's sitting room the night before. In the back of her mind she had a faint memory of walking through a gate into this garden and yet she could see no gate. But as they turned the corner to walk round the back of the house, the gate came into view. It was just as she remembered it; a tall wooden gate now blowing open and shut in the wind. As they approached the swinging gate, Ryan's curiosity got the better of him. He held the gate open and peered inside.

'Don't go in there Ryan,' warned Megan, 'it's trespassing.'

But Ryan was already inside the garden, shouting to her above the sound of the roaring wind. 'There's some big cages in here Megan … Come and look!'

Ryan was becoming very excited, but all Megan could think about was what Irene might say if she found them in her garden. She held back for a while until she could no longer resist Ryan's calls, but she wasn't prepared for what she actually saw. There were two very large animal pens in the garden. They had wooden frames with wire netting around them and roofs covered with plastic sheeting. Each pen had a strong wooden box at one end, with what looked like straw inside. The ground in the pens was grassy with a few sticks, a couple of logs and a few small rocks scattered here and there. Each had a door that was propped open. But what shocked Megan the most was the piece of red raw meat, dangling from the roof of each pen, swaying gruesomely in the wind. With their eyes transfixed on this grisly sight, Ryan and Megan moved closer to the pens, until another gust of wind slammed the gate shut again. Megan glanced round anxiously. 'We need to go Ryan,' she pleaded. But Ryan ignored her. He was still very excited, shouting even louder above the sound of the worsening storm. 'The wild cats are kept *here!*' he yelled triumphantly. 'This is where they've escaped from.'

CRASH!

They spun round as another violent gust of wind blew over two large bins by the back door. They only turned away for a split second, but that was all it took for the wild cat to spring over the gate and land softly inside the garden.

Underneath the roar of the wind, Megan and Ryan heard a deep, low growl. The cat was standing in front of the wooden gate. They were trapped.

This cat was far bigger than the one in the watchtower. It was a tawny colour with a big bushy striped tail and a large head. Its round eyes glowed pale golden yellow as it fixed them with a chilling stare and hissed at them with a blood red mouth.

There was no time to lose. They had to find somewhere to hide. Ryan grabbed Megan's arm and pulled her away from the pens, towards Irene's back door. He tried the door handle, but it was locked. There was nowhere else to go, so they dived for shelter behind the fallen bins, dragging them close for protection. And all the time the cat continued with its low menacing growl, as the wind whirled in torrents around the pens.

It seemed a long time before the cat began to move, but when it did, it moved slowly and purposefully towards one of the pens. Then it stopped and looked around with its piercing eyes. It seemed to Megan like everything was happening in slow motion. Then without warning, the cat sprang into one of the pens. Making a lunge for the piece of raw meat on the string, it wrestled the gruesome mass to the ground and began to rip the flesh apart with its long, sharp teeth. Megan's skin tingled with fear and she began to shake uncontrollably. Ryan was trying to be brave, but didn't know what to do. He took out his phone. 'Shall I call the police?'

Megan was horrified. 'No. We'll get into trouble. My dad won't cope with it.'

Ryan became irritated 'Well we're already in deep trouble now, aren't we?' he said.

'Who shall I call then, if it's not the police? You tell me and I'll call them!'

Their voices rose above the moaning wind as they became locked in an argument about who Ryan should phone, until the sound of an approaching car caused them to stop. They looked hopefully towards the back door of the gatehouse and waited. Megan let out a sigh of relief when they finally saw Irene's face at the window by the back door. Ryan sprang up, waving frantically. The next thing they heard was the back door opening and Irene's angry voice drifting on the wind. 'Get in here,' she ordered. Then, throwing only a brief glance at the cat, she ushered them into her house and closed the door.

All they could do was apologise to Irene and try to explain how they ended up in her garden. She was angry at first, but she seemed to calm down a little when Megan explained how Ryan had been trying to save the cat in the watchtower. She listened with interest when Ryan told her about the bag under the wooden seat, but she remained silent until they had finished.

'Thank you for telling me everything,' she said at last, 'but I don't want you jumping to the wrong conclusions.' She looked at her watch. 'I'll have to talk to you later. If what you say is true, I need to get to the watchtower to rescue the cat as soon as possible.'

Ryan was keen to find out more. 'Do the big cats belong to you?' he asked.

'They are not technically big cats,' she answered, 'even though they look like they are. They're called wild cats. Nobody really owns them, because they're wild, but I do try to look after them.'

'How did you come to have them?' asked Ryan again.

Irene was reluctant to talk. 'My late husband was trying to breed them,' she said quickly. 'Look I need to get to the watchtower.'

But before Irene could say any more, a loud crashing sound from the garden sent her rushing towards the window. The wind had detached a large piece of roofing felt from her shed and was hurling it across the garden. Irene headed for the back door and Ryan dashed after her.

Megan was about to follow them when something caught her eye. The little photo on the shelf that she had tried to look at the night before had something familiar about it. As she approached it to take a closer look, her heart gave a sudden leap in her chest. The woman in the photo was her mother and she was the child sitting next to her. Even though her mother had died when she was six years old, Megan recognised her mother's red curly hair. It was the same as hers. In the photograph, Megan was sitting with her mother next to a shelf full of cat ornaments and in her tiny hands she was holding a basket of knitted cats. Megan didn't know why she did it, but she slipped the tiny photograph into her pocket and then turned to look out of the window, as if she had never taken it.

She could see Ryan and Irene struggling to catch hold of the roofing felt, but there was no sign of the cat. She watched as they finally caught the huge piece of felt and tried to weigh it down with loose bricks. She knew she should go out to help them, but somehow she couldn't move. A strange sensation had come over her that rooted her to the spot. In her mind, she could hear her mother talking: *Sit here with me Megan. You hold the cats. That's it. Smile. Good girl. That'll be a lovely photo.*

It was their noisy return that finally jarred Megan back to real life. Irene complained about the wind and the damage to her shed, and Ryan began to relate how he nearly dropped a brick on his foot in the chaos. But Megan hardly heard them. Her mind was elsewhere.

When Irene finally sat down in her big armchair she looked concerned. 'Maybe I'd better wait for this wind to die down a bit, before I try to get the cat back from the watchtower,' she said.

'Good idea,' said Ryan. He seemed delighted for another opportunity to find out more.

'Did you get the cats from Scotland?' he asked.

Irene smiled. 'I can see you've done some research. Yes, my late husband Mike had a cousin there.'

When Megan heard the name Mike, she instantly knew he was the man standing by the sports car in the photo on the wall. She couldn't remember exactly when, but she knew she had met him before.

Ryan was still seeking more information. 'How did you catch the cats if they're wild?' he asked.

'Mike's cousin found a wild kitten that had been abandoned by its mother,' explained Irene. 'It was a male tom-cat and it was a vicious little thing. His cousin couldn't cope with it and was going to have it put down, but Mike took pity on it. Everyone warned him that wild cats can never be tamed, but he wouldn't listen. I wasn't having that ferocious cat in the house, so he built a pen in the garden to keep it in.'

Ryan was fascinated. 'Which cat was that? The one outside or the one in the watchtower?'

'It's the one you saw outside,' she replied. 'He's getting old now, slowing down a bit. We couldn't think what to call him so we just called him Tom.'

'Did Mike tame him?' asked Ryan.

'Oh no,' she grinned. 'You'll never convince a wild cat that you're not their enemy, but he did get Tom used to being around humans. I'm pretty sure he wouldn't attack anyone, unless he felt threatened for any reason,' she added, 'or if someone tried to take his food.' Irene chuckled. 'I leave food out for him in the pen over the winter and he always manages to return for it. Tom really loves his food.'

Megan was still only half listening. As she fingered the little silver photo frame in her pocket, thoughts of her mother were sweeping through her mind like the wind before an approaching storm.

Irene seemed pleased that Ryan was interested in her story and she directed most of her talking to him, without really noticing the increasingly troubled look on Megan's face.

'Mike enjoyed the challenge of trying to tame Tom,' she continued, 'even though he never succeeded. Then the year before Mike died, he decided he wanted to breed wild cats and create a family of them here in Oakton woods.'

'I thought it was against the law to keep big cats as pets,' interrupted Ryan.

'It is,' said Irene, 'but as I said before, they're not classed as big cats, even though male cats like Tom can grow to be the size of a small cougar. And besides,' she went on, 'Mike didn't want to keep wild cats as pets. He just wanted to keep the species going. He loved to see them running wild and free.'

Ryan was becoming more and more enthralled by Irene's story. 'Is that why Mike got the other cat?' he said excitedly, 'so they could breed?'

Irene nodded. 'We got her from a zoo that was closing down. She was only a year old when we got her. They called her

Zoe. We built another pen to keep her in, so she and Tom could get used to each other.'

She lowered her voice. 'When Mike died I wanted to carry on trying to breed the cats, because that's what he would have wanted.'

There was a pause as Irene became temporarily lost in thought, but it was Megan who finally brought the conversation to a close. She couldn't catch her breath. Her head was spinning round so fast that she thought she was going to faint. She darted up from her chair and then, as if her body and mind could withhold no more, she let out a cry of such deep despair that tears sprang from her eyes and ran down her cheeks in rivulets. Thoughts of her mother had finally overwhelmed her, like a great tidal wave.

Irene leapt up and guided Megan back to the chair. 'What's wrong Megan? Was it the cat that scared you?' Megan nodded as she continued to sob. She felt embarrassed that she couldn't control her feelings after all these years. When she had one of these panic attacks, she would tell people she wasn't well or make something else up. Being scared of the cat was as good an excuse as any.

Ryan felt guilty and ashamed. 'It's all my fault,' he said quietly. 'I'm really sorry.'

Megan looked up. She was trying to stop crying by blowing her nose hard on a tissue.

'It's OK Ryan.'

Irene thought it would do Megan good if they carried on to the café at the Hall as they had planned. She assured them that Tom would do them no harm as long as they left him alone, but Ryan wanted to know what Irene was going to do about Zoe.

'I've been letting her free to roam the woods for the last month,' she answered, 'but she always came back to the pen at night for food. So, when she didn't return all last week, I went out to look for her.'

Megan was trying desperately to regain her composure, so no-one would suspect why she had been crying. 'Is that who you were calling when you found me last night?' she asked.

'Yes, that's right,' said Irene. 'I thought the night time was the best time to find her, as she would be out hunting for food. Then I heard the screeching sound. Female wild cats can make that kind of sound when they're in need of help or looking for a mate. I had some meat in my bag to tempt her to come towards me if I found her, but of course I never thought of looking inside the watchtower.'

'How are you going to get her out?' asked Ryan.

'I've got a large cat box that she's been in before,' she replied. 'It's a bit like a cage, but I think I can carry it to the watchtower. She knows my voice so if she can move at all, I'll lure her into that with some meat.'

'What about the bag under the seat?' asked Ryan. 'Can you find out what's in it?'

Irene gave a concerned look. 'If there *is* anything valuable in it, I will have to take it to the police. Assuming I can reach it that is.'

She looked out of the window. 'The wind seems to be dying down a little bit, so maybe I'll go now,' she said.

As they left, Ryan asked Irene if they could call in to see her on the way back. He said he wanted to find out if Zoe had been rescued, but Megan guessed he was probably more interested in the bag. Irene hastened them to the back door and out into the garden.

'If I'm not here when you return,' she called from the doorway, 'I'll still be at the watchtower. Come and find me there.'

4

Frog-Eyed Sprite

It was a pleasant walk down to the Hall. The track was narrow, but it was well trodden by walkers and easy to follow and they were thankful that the wind had eased a little. Ryan talked excitedly about what might be in the bag in the watchtower. He had lots of wild ideas ranging from smuggled jewellery to ancient treasure from Oakton Hall and he was fascinated by how the bag could have got inside the watchtower if the iron gate was locked. Megan wasn't really paying attention. She was thinking about the photo in her pocket and wondering why Irene had pretended not to know who she was last night. She decided that the only way to find out was to ask her dad, but she didn't look forward to broaching the subject with him. Whenever she mentioned her mother, her dad got upset. Megan had always wanted to know more about how her mother died, but her dad wouldn't talk about it. She knew that her mother was killed in a car crash somewhere off the York Road, but she knew very little else because, for some reason, she couldn't find anyone who would talk to her about it. As the Hall came into view, Megan shelved her thoughts and put her feelings away for later, as if in a box. That was something she was well used to doing.

The Hall was a majestic sight, standing proudly in the middle of a small lake surrounded by trees and ornamental gardens. They had to walk through a small car park to reach the narrow iron bridge leading to the Hall. There were only a few cars in the car park and one car stood out from the others. It was a small red classic sports car, with a soft top. Ryan headed towards it to take a closer look. 'Very cool,' he drooled. 'I wonder who this belongs to.'

Megan joined him. 'I don't know,' she replied, 'but Kirsty was telling everyone at the swimming club that she had a new car and I think she said it was red.'

Ryan smoothed his hand over the car bonnet like he was stroking a cat. 'It's a Sprite,' he said.

'Yeah. That's right,' said Megan confidently. 'It's called a Frog-Eyed Sprite, because the two big headlights on the bonnet stick out like a frog's eyes.'

Ryan was impressed. 'How do you know that?'

Megan had no idea how she knew about this car. 'I must have seen one before somewhere,' she replied vaguely.

Ryan moved round to peer through the windows. 'Does Kirsty smoke?' he asked.

Megan shrugged her shoulders. 'I don't know. Why?'

'There's a packet of cigarettes on the passenger seat,' said Ryan casually.

They were still admiring the car, when they heard someone calling. 'Megan. Hey Megan!'

A woman with two children came over the bridge, waving as they walked. It was Mrs Campbell, one of Megan's neighbours, with her two young daughters, Esther and Ivy.

'Hi Megan. We've been swimming in the new pool,' they called.

Megan loved these little girls. They always seemed so happy. Mrs Campbell and the girls gave Megan a lift to swimming club every Saturday, so she knew them quite well. She had been going to Oakton swimming club for a while now and it was one of the few places her dad would let her go without him. She envied the two little girls having each other, and a mother to go swimming with.

Mrs Campbell looked very serious. 'Did you know Mrs Harris across the road was burgled last night?'

'We saw the police car,' said Ryan.

'Mrs Harris was crying wasn't she Mummy?' said Esther sadly. 'They took her grandma's ring.'

'We're going to get her some flowers today,' said Ivy.

'I hear the Hall was burgled as well the other week,' said Mrs Campbell. 'Sarah on reception told me they're having to change some locks, because someone stole a bunch of keys.'

'Come on Mummy,' called Ivy as she ran around chasing after her sister.

Mrs Campbell went to gather them up. 'OK girls, let's go and get the flowers. Bye Megan.'

Megan was intrigued about what they had just heard. 'Maybe one of the stolen keys was for the watchtower,' she said as they headed for the Hall.

'Maybe it was stolen by someone who works there,' said Ryan.

The café at the Hall overlooked the lake, but from some parts of the café you could also see down into the gym. Megan went to the counter to buy the drinks and cakes, whilst Ryan found a table. By the time Megan arrived with the tray of food, Ryan was looking towards the gym with great interest. 'That looks like Kirsty lifting weights down there,' he said.

Megan took the food off the tray and glanced into the gym. 'Yeah that's her.'

Ryan picked up his cake, but his eyes were still focused on Kirsty. 'She must be really strong,' he noted. 'Look at the size of those weights.'

They both watched in awe as she lifted weight after weight, her slim body writhing with effort as she hauled each weight above her head with determined precision.

'It must be carrying that heavy backpack around that's

given her all that strength,' said Ryan sarcastically. Even though he had only met her once in the woods, he had seen her running around the village on numerous occasions and there was something about her manner that he didn't like. 'I wonder how she managed to afford that sports car,' he sneered.

Megan ignored him. She didn't really know Kirsty, but she quite liked her. She was one of the many people who had come to work at Oakton Hall Leisure Centre, since a new company took it over several months ago.

They had just finished eating when Kirsty arrived in the café. Megan beckoned her over. 'I'm just showing Ryan round,' she said. Kirsty grinned at them both. 'If you've not been to the new pool yet, I'm on my way there now,' she said. 'You can watch me take a lesson if you like, but I'm in a hurry, so you'll have to be quick.'

Megan jumped up to join her, followed by a reluctant Ryan.

'I'll take you round the back of the kitchens, its quicker,' said Kirsty, still smiling.

A side door saying 'Staff Only' led them to the outside, revealing a panoramic view of the lake with ducks and swans gliding across the water. They followed Kirsty along a small pathway until they came to a grassy area with a large stone on a plinth. The stone had some kind of metal dial on it. 'That's a sundial,' explained Kirsty. 'There are lots of things like that around the grounds here. They were put in by the Squire who built the Hall.'

'Like the watchtower in the woods,' said Ryan quickly. 'I expect you go past there a lot when you go running don't you Kirsty?' he remarked. 'Do staff have a key to that tower? If you had a key, you could go in there for a rest or even store things in it.'

Megan gave him a disapproving look, but Kirsty just laughed. She seemed unphased by Ryan's strange remarks.

Turning a corner brought them to the back of the kitchens,

where a man in a white apron was stubbing a cigarette out on the ground with his shoe. Megan noticed he had a mop of curly hair which was so jet black that it looked like he had dyed it. The man hadn't seen them coming and jumped as Kirsty scolded him. 'Joe Hawkins. I thought you were giving that up,' she quipped.

The man swung round angrily. He looked shocked when he saw Megan and Ryan and stared at them strangely. 'Who's this?' he asked nervously.

'This is Megan, and Ryan,' laughed Kirsty. 'Did we make you jump? We're on our way to the pool.' Moving closer to face him, Kirsty leaned over and pushed a red cigarette packet further down into his shirt pocket, so it was out of sight. 'Don't let the boss see that,' she warned.

'I don't care. I'm leaving next week anyway,' replied Joe, still staring at Megan and Ryan.

'Might see you later if you're out running,' said Kirsty. 'Come on you two. I'm already late.'

Joe followed them with his eyes as they walked past him and on towards the pool. Megan felt she had seen Joe somewhere before, but she couldn't remember where.

'If Sarah finds out he's been smoking at work there'll be trouble,' said Kirsty when they were out of earshot. 'Even if he has only got a week to go. He's promised her he'll cut down.'

'Do you mean Sarah who works on reception?' asked Megan. 'Is she Joe's girlfriend?'

'No. She's his wife,' said Kirsty. 'They have a little girl. She's really cute.'

Kirsty led them back into the leisure centre through a side door leading to a long corridor.

'Do you smoke Kirsty?' asked Ryan as they walked.

'Definitely not,' she replied, 'and if Joe doesn't stop smoking soon he won't have enough breath for that marathon he keeps telling everyone he's training for. Sarah says he often goes running in the middle of the night, because he can't sleep, which is a bit stupid if you ask me.'

'That's crazy,' said Megan.

'Yeah, that sums Joe up really,' laughed Kirsty. 'A bit crazy.'

When they reached the entrance to the changing rooms, Kirsty stopped. 'Do you want to watch my lesson? I'll be finished in about half an hour. Then I can show you how to use the new climbing wall if you want.'

'No thanks,' said Ryan rather too quickly. 'We've got to get back.'

Kirsty was still smiling when she left them, but Megan was becoming irritated by Ryan's rudeness. She felt like walking away, but she knew her dad wouldn't want her to go home alone. She had also promised to show Ryan round all the facilities, so despite her feelings, she decided to carry on.

'Now you've seen the pool, do you think you'll join the swimming club?' asked Megan as they made their way out.

Ryan shook his head. 'Not if Kirsty's the swimming coach.'

'What's so wrong with Kirsty?' asked Megan.

'She's just too cheerful and in your face all the time,' said Ryan. 'I can't stand people like that.'

Megan sighed. 'They do have other teachers as well as Kirsty you know.'

'I just like to swim on my own really,' said Ryan, 'and anyway I don't have much spare time for swimming.'

'Well what do you do with yourself at weekends then, if you have no time for swimming?' asked Megan.

'I have a lot of school work to do and I take Skippy out for walks,' he replied defensively, 'but I don't know why I need to tell *you* what I do.'

Megan was annoyed by his attitude. She was beginning to see a side of him that she disliked. 'When do you see your parents then?' she asked.

'My dad comes to see me when he has the time!' he said bitterly. 'But he has to work longer hours to get enough money, so he can finish our new house.'

Megan was curious. 'Why don't you go to the house at weekends? Don't they want you to help?'

'I don't want to go,' he answered angrily. 'I'd rather just take Skippy out for walks or watch TV.'

Megan realised that she didn't know much about Ryan's family, except that his dad was called Andy and they'd moved up from London to build a house in a nearby village.

'Don't you miss your mum and dad?' asked Megan rather bluntly.

Ryan's off-hand reaction took her by surprise. 'I couldn't care less!' he snapped. 'Let's get back to Irene's. I want to see if she's got the cat out of the watchtower.'

As Ryan strode away, Megan wished she hadn't asked so many questions. They walked back over the bridge without speaking until the sudden arrival of a police car in the car park prompted Megan to speak again. 'Do you think they're investigating the burglary at the Hall?'

'Who knows,' said Ryan. 'They haven't arrested anyone for the other burglaries yet have they?'

Two police officers got out of their car and walked slowly across the iron bridge as Megan and Ryan set off back to the gatehouse.

The wind had dropped completely by the time they arrived at Irene's house and there was a strange stillness in the woods. They noticed that Irene's gate was still open and the bins were still on their sides. It looked like she had left in a hurry. They were relieved to find the pens were empty and there was no sign of the cat. The big black car was still parked outside, but as no-one answered when they knocked on the gatehouse door, they made their way towards the watchtower.

They were half-way up the track that ran behind the bench, when they met Irene. She was on her way down, struggling to carry a large box-cage. It was covered with a cloth, but they knew by the low growl coming from within, that she had managed to rescue Zoe. Ryan reached out to take hold of one side of the cage. 'Watch out!' cried Irene. 'Her claws can extend through the wire. That's why I've got the cloth over it.'

After much growling and hissing from Zoe, Irene and Ryan managed to manoeuvre the cage so they could carry it safely together. But the track was steep and narrow and it was slow going. Once they reached the wider, flatter path by the bench, the cage became much easier to carry.

'How did you get Zoe into the cage?' asked Ryan.

Irene looked relieved to be on firmer ground. 'Zoe knows this cage well,' she explained, 'and she knows my voice too, so it was something familiar for her. And besides, I think she was so hungry that she dragged herself into the cage to get at the meat in there. Her leg looks like it's stopped bleeding, but she may have broken a bone.'

'What about the bag?' asked Megan.

Irene shook her head. 'I couldn't reach it.'

Ryan looked disappointed.

'But then I got a stick,' she went on, 'and I managed to drag something out, but I didn't have time to see if I could reach the rest.' She nodded towards the bag on her shoulder. 'It's in here,' she added. 'I'll show you when we get back.'

Ryan's eagerness to find out what was in the bag made him try to walk a little faster, but it wasn't easy carrying the cage and it took some time to reach the gatehouse.

With more snarling and spitting from Zoe, they eased the large cage first through Irene's front door and then through the kitchen door, until they finally placed it on the kitchen floor.

When Irene took the cover off the cage, the cat leapt up with a hiss, clinging to the top part of the wire with her huge claws, but then sank down again almost immediately. There was a thin trickle of blood coming from her nose. Irene gasped at the sight of it and put the cloth back over the cage. 'I think she'll calm down better in the dark,' she said anxiously. 'She's just had some meat, so let's leave her in peace for a while. I'll take a closer look at her later.'

They moved into the sitting room and talked about what might be wrong with Zoe. Irene thought the cat's leg would eventually heal, but she feared she might have got pneumonia after spending so many nights in the cold without enough food. However, as the conversation went on, she became a little more optimistic. 'I'll put some straw inside the cage for bedding and keep the heating on tonight,' she said thoughtfully. 'A few days in a warm room with some proper food and water will hopefully do the trick. Then I'll put her in one of the pens. She still has some spark left in her, so that's a good sign.'

Ryan was interested in the cat, but he was more interested in what Irene had recovered from the bag. 'Can we look inside?' he said pointing to Irene's shoulder bag.

Irene took out a strip of brightly coloured ribbon with a small disc attached to the end of it. Handling it carefully, she placed it on a nearby coffee table. 'Don't touch it!' she warned. 'Not unless you want the police to find your fingerprints all over it when I take it to the station. My prints will be on it, because I found it, but it's best if you two don't get involved.'

They both nodded in agreement and hung back. Ryan was looking thoughtful. 'I think I might know who this belongs to,' he said gravely. 'My grandad's friend Mary was burgled some time ago. They stole some jewellery, but they also stole her grandad's war medals.'

Irene turned the disc over in her hand. 'Yes. It's a First World War medal,' she said. 'I think this is the type that everyone got if they were in the war, so I don't think it's worth a fortune, but it will mean a lot to someone.'

She turned to look directly at Megan. 'We need to reunite people with the things that are precious to them, don't we Megan?' she said pointedly. 'Things like medals and photographs are sometimes all we have left to remind us of people who are no longer with us.'

Irene's stare made Megan feel uncomfortable. She felt a pang of guilt. She guessed that Irene knew she had taken the photograph from the shelf. Otherwise she would not have spoken directly to her in that way.

Megan slowly took the photograph from her coat pocket and handed it back to Irene.

'Sorry,' she murmured faintly as Irene gently took it from her and replaced it on the shelf.

'I just want to know why you have a photo of me and my mother in your house.'

Ryan looked shocked. He knew nothing at all about what was going on.

Irene's face darkened. 'I'm really sorry Megan, but your father asked me not to talk to you about your mother,' she said shakily. 'He said he would tell you what happened when you were old enough.'

A pain swelled up in Megan's stomach as the frustration began to take hold. 'What do you mean "What happened?",' she cried. 'I thought she died in a car crash. That's what my dad told me.'

Irene's words were calm, but her face betrayed her panic. 'Yes, she did. But …'

'But what?' Megan's voice was high pitched as she struggled to catch her breath. 'Why will no-one tell me exactly what happened?' she blurted out angrily. 'I'm nearly thirteen. Surely I'm old enough to know by now, aren't I?'

'You need to talk to your dad,' was all Irene would say, as she hurriedly left the room before anyone could see her wipe away the solitary tear that fell from her eye.

It felt to Megan like a gunshot had pierced her heart, stunning her into an uneasy silence. With shaking legs, she sank down into the chair by the shelf. Something was happening to her that had never happened before. Strange new memories were beginning to seep back into her consciousness. She remembered running out of a gate into some woods and she remembered someone calling: '*Megan, where are you? It's not safe to hide in the woods. Megan. Megan!*'

'Are you OK Megan?' Ryan's voice brought her back to reality as Irene came into the room and put the medal in a plastic bag. She spoke as if nothing had happened. 'I'll take this to the police station later, after I've made Zoe more comfortable,' she said. 'But don't worry, I won't mention you two.'

'Thank you,' mumbled Ryan awkwardly.

'It's me that should thank you for looking after Zoe and telling me where to find her,' said Irene. She took a sideways look at Megan, who was still staring at the shelf. Megan had a sick feeling rising in her stomach, but she tried to keep calm and stay quiet in the hope that it would soon go away.

Ryan moved towards the front door. He felt so uncomfortable with everything that had happened – he just wanted to leave as quickly as possible.

'Just one thing before you go,' said Irene anxiously. 'No-one must find out there are wild cats in these woods. Otherwise they'll be in danger. You must promise to keep their existence a secret.' She looked at them gravely. 'Please,' she added.

They both nodded.

'Thank you,' she said, as she followed them to the door. 'I hope I can trust you.'

5

Fire

So much had happened in such a short space of time that it was difficult for Megan and Ryan to talk as they walked home. Although Ryan was intrigued to find out more about Megan's mother, he didn't want to upset Megan by asking her questions. He was also still thinking about the wild cats and wondering about the bag in the watchtower.

Neither of them spoke until they arrived outside Ryan's house. Ryan noticed that the lounge curtains in Megan's house were closed.

'Is your dad out?' he asked.

'No,' said Megan trying to sound casual. 'He often likes to sit in the dark. I expect he's got the TV on.' She moved quickly towards her gate, hoping he wouldn't ask any more questions.

'Do you want to come with me tomorrow?' asked Ryan suddenly. 'I'm taking Skippy for a walk in the woods. We could have another look at that bag in the tower.'

Megan's first thought was that Ryan was only saying that to make her feel better, but the thought of getting away from her dad, even for a short time, was becoming very attractive. 'OK,' she said trying not to sound too keen. 'I'll ask my dad. He might let me go, now he's met you.'

'I'll call for you about ten,' said Ryan as they parted.

Megan had forgotten to take the spare key, so she knocked on the door and waited. When she heard her dad shuffling along the polished hallway in his old slippers, she felt a pang of guilt. At that moment in time, she actually wanted to be somewhere else; anywhere else. She wanted to slow everything down, so she could stand outside her door for ever and never have to go inside.

As soon as her dad opened the door, she could tell by his face that he was in one of his silent moods. She'd had enough practice at trying to read him. Megan was scared of these silences. It made her think that it must be her fault. It made her think that she had done something terribly wrong, even though she didn't know what it could be. There was a time when she would try to snap her dad out of it by chatting to him and asking him questions, but she found his one word answers so exhausting that she eventually gave up.

She went into the kitchen and tried to distract herself by emptying the washing machine. Thankfully the blood stains had come out of her coat and glove, so she hung them over the radiator to dry.

She looked in the freezer to see what they might have to eat. There was a time when she was younger when her dad used to cook. He wasn't very good at it, but he used to make the effort. Now he didn't seem to care about anything. She pulled out a couple of frozen meals and put them in the microwave. She couldn't remember if her mum was a good cook or not, but she always thought that things would surely be a lot better if her mum was still alive.

Megan put her dad's meal on a tray and took it to him in the lounge. He was sitting in his chair, staring at the fire. She said nothing as she handed him the tray. She had learnt not to challenge the silences. Sitting alone at the kitchen table, she nibbled at her food. She didn't feel much like eating.

When she went to collect her dad's tray she was pleased to see he had eaten the meal, because sometimes, when he was like this, he would refuse to eat. Even though she hated these silent spells, it sometimes worked to her advantage. Her dad was less inclined to make a fuss about things when he was like this. He barely nodded when she asked him if she could go out with Ryan again in the morning and that at least gave her something to look forward to.

Megan went to bed early that night, but found it hard to sleep. She kept thinking about Irene and wondering why there were so many secrets surrounding the death of her mother. She decided to take a look inside the memory box that she kept on her bedside table. It had things in it that reminded her of her mother. She wondered if something in there might give her some information. Was there something she had missed over the years? Along with the many photos in the box, there were some personal items that belonged to her mother like a silver bangle, a small opal ring and a book that her mum used to read to her when she was a baby. Then there were the birthday cards from long ago. Some were home-made cards that Megan had sent to her mother with childish drawings on the front and lots of crooked kisses. But there was one card that she had always wondered about. It was a birthday card from both her parents, sent to Megan on her seventh birthday. She always thought this was strange, because her dad told her she was only six when her mum died. She was always meaning to ask her dad about it, but she never seemed to find the right moment. A wave of tiredness suddenly came over her. The day had been quite eventful and she needed time to rest. She yawned as she put the box back on her bedside table and snuggled under her duvet.

Megan got up early the next morning. She wanted to make sure she was ready for Ryan. By 9.30 a.m. she had made her breakfast, washed up and cleaned the bathroom and been to see if the post had arrived. There was no post as yet, but lying on the doormat was a handwritten letter without a stamp. It was addressed to her dad, so Megan took it to him in the lounge.

He looked at it with a puzzled expression, but then put it to one side. 'I'll open it later,' he said. Her dad seemed a little more communicative this morning, but Megan was still worried he might change his mind about letting her go out with Ryan, so she didn't want to stress him by asking him about the letter. She was relieved when he made no comment as she left the house.

When she stepped outside, the cold blast of winter air took Megan's breath away, but she felt exhilarated, like a caged animal allowed to be free. Ryan was waiting for her with Skippy straining on the lead. The old dog still had some energy when it came to walks and she barked with excitement as they set off towards the woods. It crossed Megan's mind that the girls at school would be teasing her if they knew she was going out with the boy next door. She never met up with any of them out of school, so they were always asking her if she had a secret boyfriend. She was thankful that none of them lived nearby.

Ryan also looked better for a night's sleep. 'My dad rang me last night,' he announced cheerfully. 'He's having problems with the electrics in our new house, but he said it shouldn't be too long before we can move into at least part of it.'

Megan was surprised at how upset she felt at the thought of Ryan leaving. Despite the fact she'd found him very annoying at times yesterday, she was beginning to enjoy having someone her own age living next door, even if it was a boy.

'I bet your mum will be pleased,' said Megan politely.

Ryan scowled. 'My mum doesn't live with us any more,' he said quietly. 'My parents got divorced a few years ago. I've got a step-mum now.'

Megan was shocked. 'So where's your real mum?'

Ryan looked uncomfortable. 'She's moved to America,' he replied irritably. 'Which means I won't be seeing much of her now.'

Megan couldn't imagine having a mother and not being able to see her, but she sensed that Ryan didn't want to talk about his family anymore, so she changed the subject.

'How far are we going?' she asked as they turned onto the woodland path. Ryan was visibly relaxed. 'I thought we could take another look in the watchtower,' he said. 'We could get a stick and see if we could pull that bag towards us.'

Megan wasn't so sure. 'Maybe we shouldn't do that if Irene's going to the police about it.' But Ryan was not to be deterred. 'We're not doing anything wrong, are we? I can tell the police it was me who found the bag if you're worried about your dad finding out.'

As they approached the woodland path, Megan finally relented. 'OK, but I'm not touching it,' she warned.

Ryan waited until they were well into the woods before letting Skippy off the lead. They smiled as they watched her gamboling about like a puppy for a few minutes, before slowing down to her usual stately pace.

As they came within sight of the bench they saw two people wearing hooded jackets walking away from them in the distance, but otherwise it was quiet. It wasn't until they were actually at the bench that they both looked up towards the path leading to the watchtower and froze. Clouds of smoke were billowing though the sky. Megan looked around her. The woods were empty. The two people they had seen in the distance were now out of sight and there was no-one about to help.

'That smoke's coming from near the watchtower,' said Ryan. 'The woods could be on fire. We'd better call the fire brigade.' As he took out his phone, he looked around for Skippy. She was nowhere to be seen. 'Skippy! Where are you?' he called urgently.

Megan gave a shout and pointed up the track. Skippy was chasing something and she was running towards the smoke. They didn't stop to think. They just ran after her. 'Skippy!' they shouted frantically. 'Skippy come back.'

As they drew nearer the watchtower, the smoke became thicker and the heat became more intense. It was becoming more difficult to breathe. The fire seemed to be spreading rapidly through the pine trees, cutting deeper into the heart of the woods. Ryan glanced through the acrid smoke towards the watchtower. He couldn't be certain, but it looked as if the iron gate was open. 'Skippy!' he yelled again, 'Skippy!'.

Then a voice came out of the smoke. 'Get back! Go back!' It was Kirsty. She was holding Skippy by the collar. 'I've rung the fire brigade. You can't do anything. Just go back!' she called.

Ryan lunged forward and snatched Skippy from her hands. There was no time to say any more, but out of the corner of his eye, he spotted another red cigarette packet, lying on the ground. He put the whimpering dog back on the lead and they headed back down the track.

The choking smoke stung their throats and burned their eyes as the fire devoured the woods. All they could do was run. They ran with all the other creatures in the woods, like a great avalanche moving down a mountain.

Kirsty was in front with Megan close behind, followed by Ryan, who was now holding Skippy in his arms like a baby. The old dog was trembling with fear and he couldn't risk losing her again. They were about half-way down the track when something crashed through the branches nearby and the faint sound of a low growl could be heard behind the crackling of the fire. Skippy let out a long howl, but only Ryan and Megan turned to look. In the shadows of the burning pine trees, two golden eyes looked at them through the smoke. Tom had returned to look for Zoe.

Ryan couldn't say whether it was the sighting of Tom that caused him to fall, because it all happened so quickly. One minute he was on the track and the next minute he was lying on the ground in agony, with his ankle twisted underneath him. Skippy had jumped free, but was now whining and licking his face. When Megan and Kirsty tried to help Ryan to his feet, he cried out in such pain that they had to stop. Megan looked at Kirsty. 'What shall we do?' she cried. But Kirsty was beginning to panic. Her face was full of terror and her hands were shaking uncontrollably. 'Ryan, you have to move!' she shrieked. 'You have to get up. Get up Ryan! Get up!'

Megan stooped down beside Ryan. She knew she had to keep calm. 'Put your arm round my shoulder Ryan,' she said firmly. 'Kirsty, you get the other side of him and we'll get him to stand up.' Kirsty did as she was told, but when Ryan cried out in pain as he stood up, she let him go. 'Let's try again Kirsty,' said Megan. 'We've got to get out of here.'

Ryan braced himself for the forthcoming pain. The flames were getting nearer by the minute and he knew it. Megan did her best to keep hold of Skippy's lead as they helped Ryan down the track. Ryan did his best to keep going, but by the time they reached the bench, he was beginning to feel faint.

It was at this point that Kirsty began behaving even more strangely. She threw her arms round Skippy's neck and began to cry hysterically. The old dog trembled and looked at Ryan with her soft brown eyes, but she didn't move. It was as if she was grateful for the comfort.

Megan didn't know what to do, so she just waited. She waited until Kirsty's tears subsided and then watched as Kirsty tied Skippy's lead to the bench.

'Sorry,' she sniffed as she bent down to look at Ryan's ankle. 'Can you move your toes?'

Ryan didn't reply. He wasn't sure if he could move anything

He was grateful for Kirsty's help, but her strange behaviour made him feel uneasy.

Kirsty sat beside them on the bench, as Ryan nursed his throbbing ankle. 'The fire brigade should be here soon,' she said, as if trying to reassure herself.

They sat in silence for a few moments before Kirsty spoke again. She seemed to be making an effort to get back to her usual self. 'I'm sure it's only a sprained ankle Ryan,' she said breezily, 'but we need to get you both home. I would take you in my car, but it's in the car park at the Hall and you'll never walk that far.'

Ryan looked surprised. 'Three of us wouldn't get into your two-seater sports car,' he scoffed. Kirsty looked puzzled. 'What do you mean? I've not got a...'. The wailing sound of a siren in the distance told them that the fire engine was on its way.

'You need to stay here Kirsty,' said Megan. 'You need to tell the fire brigade what you saw.' Kirsty nodded weakly. She was beginning to look deflated again. 'I'll go and get Irene,' said Megan. 'She lives in one of the gatehouses. She can help me get Ryan to her house and then maybe she'll drive us home.'

'OK,' said Kirsty. 'I'll stay here with Ryan 'til you come back.'

Ryan didn't look too pleased, but he was in no position to argue.

Megan sprinted towards Irene's gatehouse as fast as she could. When she saw Irene's car outside, she banged on the door, but it was some time before Irene appeared. She had been trying to get some bedding into Zoe's cage, but Zoe kept on trying to attack her. When Irene finally opened the door, Megan burst into the hallway. 'The woods are on fire!' she gasped. 'Ryan's hurt his ankle and can't walk. Can you come and help him? Can you take us home in your car?'

Irene was stunned. 'Slow down Megan. Tell me again. What's happened?'

As Megan became a little calmer, she was able to explain

to Irene exactly why Ryan needed her help and it wasn't long before they were both on their way back to the bench, armed with a small ice pack and a bandage.

Megan raced ahead. She was wanting to get Ryan home as quickly as possible, but she was also worried about what her dad would say if she was late home. Irene called after her. 'Slow down Maggie… er… Megan. I'm sure Ryan will be fine.'

It was just one mistake. It was just one little word, but it tore through Megan's body like an electric shock. She stopped to let Irene catch up. 'You just called me Maggie,' she said. 'That was my mum's name.'

Irene sighed deeply. 'Sorry!' she whispered. 'I knew your mum well. You look so like her that I called you Maggie by mistake. Your hair is exactly the same colour as hers. Sorry if it upset you.'

Megan swallowed hard before she spoke. She had found over the years that this was the best way to fight off any unwanted tears. 'No-one ever mentions my mum,' she said softly. 'It's as if she didn't exist.'

'Well she did exist,' said Irene reassuringly. 'She was my best friend.'

'Then why won't you tell me the truth about what happened to her?' implored Megan.

'I'm so sorry Megan, but your dad is the one who needs to tell you,' said Irene gently.

'He won't even say her name,' replied Megan. 'He can't bear to talk about her.'

Irene shook her head. 'I'm sorry,' she muttered. 'I'm so sorry.'

'Maybe you could talk to him,' said Megan. 'Maybe you could persuade him to tell me what happened.'

Irene shook her head. 'He won't speak to me.'

Megan was shocked. 'Why?'

'Because he's angry with me,' she confessed.

'Why?'

'I can't tell you that,' replied Irene. 'But I'll tell you what I will do. I'll go and see Bill. Maybe he can persuade your dad to talk to you.'

'How do you know Bill?' asked Megan.

'He used to repair Mike's vintage cars,' she said sadly.

By the time they got to the bench, a fire engine was throbbing nearby and Kirsty was talking to one of the fire crew. A few passers-by were standing in a group, looking up at the clouds of smoke still billowing above the trees. Megan recognised one of them. It was Joe. When he saw Megan, he moved towards her. 'Are you alright Megan?' he asked.

Megan thought his concern for her was surprising, considering how much worse Ryan was, but she answered politely that she was fine and moved away from him to sit next to Ryan. Megan watched as Joe had a quick word with Kirsty, before running off towards the woodyard.

'They think they've got to the fire in time,' said Kirsty, as she joined them at the bench.

'It shouldn't take long to put it out.'

'Good job you called them when you did then,' said Irene. 'Well done.'

Between them, Irene and Megan managed to strap the ice pack around Ryan's painful ankle and bandage it up firmly. He looked pale, cold and shaken.

'Now let's see if you can lean on me and stand up,' suggested Irene, but Kirsty had a better idea. 'I can carry Ryan to your house,' she said, flexing her muscles. 'I can do a fireman's lift.'

Ryan leant heavily on Irene, and struggled to stand up. 'No-one's carrying me anywhere!' he declared angrily. 'I can still hop on one leg you know.'

'OK. OK,' laughed Kirsty, but Ryan was not amused. He was suspicious of anyone who could turn on cheerfulness like a tap, but there were other reasons why he didn't trust Kirsty. Even though she said she didn't smoke, Ryan couldn't stop thinking about the cigarette packet he had seen on the ground, when they saw Kirsty at the watchtower. It was the second such packet he had found up there and it was the same brand as the one on the passenger seat of what he thought was Kirsty's Frog-Eyed Sprite.

'I'll help you walk, Ryan,' said Kirsty, 'if you won't let me carry you.'

Irene picked up Kirsty's backpack from the ground and passed it to her. 'That's heavy,' she remarked.

'It's got weights in,' explained Kirsty. 'I've got to get fit for the York marathon.'

Irene was curious. 'Are you running for charity?'

Kirsty fished in her pocket and handed Irene a leaflet. 'This tells you all about it, if you want to sponsor me,' she said. 'Come on. Ryan needs to see a doctor.'

The level path meant that they were soon outside the gatehouse, where Ryan limped painfully into Irene's car. 'Thanks for your help Kirsty,' said Megan, as they waved her goodbye, but Ryan said nothing. He didn't even look at her, because he had now convinced himself that it was Kirsty who set the woods on fire with a careless cigarette.

6

A Seventh Birthday Card

Bill was visiting Paul's house when Irene's car pulled up outside. He saw the car from Paul's lounge window and rushed to the door when he saw Ryan. Irene put down the car window. 'Hello Bill,' she said cautiously. 'Ryan's hurt his ankle. I can drive you both to the hospital if you like. It will save having to move him again.'

By now, Paul was standing at his front door, beckoning frantically for Megan to come in. His face was dark, like thunder clouds before a violent storm. Megan touched Ryan on the shoulder. 'Good luck,' she whispered. Ryan looked at Paul standing in the doorway. 'I think you might be the one who needs the luck,' he said.

Megan hoped Irene hadn't forgotten that she was going to talk to Bill, but now was not the right time to remind her. So, she took a deep breath and went to meet her father. A few minutes later, Bill got in Irene's car and they drove off to the hospital.

Paul was very agitated. One minute he was pacing round the room and the next he was sitting in his chair with his head in his hands. 'What were you doing in that woman's car?' he demanded. It wasn't easy trying to explain when her dad was like this, but Megan persisted. She always tried to keep as calm as she could, so he wouldn't get any worse. She told him they had been in the woods when they noticed some smoke and then Skippy ran away and Ryan fell. She explained that Irene's house was the nearest place to get help. She told her dad that she knew who Irene was because she had visited her school.

After a while, her explanations seemed to pacify him. 'I'm sorry,' he said suddenly. 'I'm just trying to take care of you that's all.' He walked over to where Megan was standing and put his arm round her shoulder. 'You see,' he continued, 'that woman is not someone I want you to talk to. I know she helped Ryan but she's a bad influence.'

Tempting though it was to disagree with her dad, Megan decided this was not a good time to ask about the relationship between Irene and her mother. So she just smiled, like she always did when her dad got over one of these outbursts. All she wanted was for him to be at peace. She would just have to wait for Irene to talk to Bill. Maybe then she would find out a bit more of the truth.

After making a quick meal for herself and her dad, Megan went to her room. Her dad said he was tired and would be going to bed early, but he was still downstairs when she heard the phone ring. She opened her bedroom door to listen. From what her dad was saying she could tell it was Bill on the phone. When her dad put the phone down, she dashed back to her bedroom and jumped into bed as he came upstairs.

'I'm glad you're still awake,' said Paul sitting on the end of Megan's bed. 'That was Bill on the phone. Ryan's ankle is badly sprained, but they're now on their way back from the hospital, so there's nothing to worry about.'

Megan sat up in bed and switched on her bedside light. 'That's good news,' she said.

'It is,' said Paul, 'but he won't be able to walk for a while.'

Megan was relieved that her dad appeared to have calmed down after his outburst. So, on the spur of the moment, she decided this might be a good time to try to talk to him again. She reached for the memory box on her bedside table and placed it on the bed. 'Can I ask you something Dad?' she said as she lifted the lid of the box. 'There are things in here I don't understand.'

Paul sat with his eyes downcast and braced himself, as if he was expecting pain.

'I'll be thirteen soon,' said Megan, 'and I need to know things, otherwise I'll be guessing and making things up.' She pulled out a bright pink birthday card. On the front was a picture of a teddy bear holding a box and above the box were the words *Happy 7th Birthday*. 'You said I was six years old when Mum died,' she said as she opened the card, 'but inside this card it says *Happy 7th Birthday Megan. Love from Mummy and Daddy*.'

Paul sighed and stared at the opposite wall.

'That doesn't make sense Dad,' she said softly.

It was probably only a few seconds before her dad finally spoke, but it seemed like a long time to Megan. It would have been so easy to give in; to make him feel better and take away the pain, but she held the silence. She just had to.

'I can't remember exactly what I said,' he murmured, 'but yes, you were seven years old. It happened just after your seventh birthday. Why does it matter exactly how old you were?' Paul put his head in his hands as if it was all too much to bear. Although Megan felt desperately sad, she was pleased she had dared to ask her dad a question and had found out one small piece of truth.

Spurred on by her success, she began to ask some more questions. 'I know it's not easy Dad,' she said gently, 'but I would like to know more about how Mum died.'

His reply was abrupt and swift, as if he couldn't wait to finish speaking. 'The car she was driving hit a tree near the York Road,' he said. 'We don't know why. There was nothing wrong with the car, nothing wrong with her health and no other cars were involved. That's all you need to know.' Paul stood up to leave. 'What's the point of filling your head with things you don't need to know and painful memories that will haunt you forever like they haunt me,' he cried.

Megan raised her voice in frustration. 'But I need to know the truth, whatever it is,' she blurted out. 'I mean, why did the car hit the tree? There must be a reason.'

Paul was standing by the door. His face was ashen and his eyes watery. 'Something probably distracted her,' he said as his voice became louder and louder, 'but we don't know what it was, so let's leave it there shall we. Just leave it alone Megan will you,' he shouted. 'I've had enough!'

The door banged loudly as he left the room. 'OK,' she whispered to herself. 'It's OK.' But she knew in her heart that it wasn't. Megan stroked her precious birthday card before putting it back in her memory box. She knew then that if she wanted to find out any more, she would have to find a way to talk to Irene.

That night Megan had one of her usual nightmares. Whatever was happening in her dreams, it would often involve some kind of loud bang which scared her and woke her up. When she awoke from one of these nightmares she would be crying and shaking uncontrollably, but she never called out for her dad. She always tried so hard not to upset him.

That night she had the same nightmare again, but this time there was a difference. This time the loud bang that woke her up was real. She sat up and looked at the clock. It was 1 a.m. Then she heard the sound again. It was the unmistakable sound of breaking glass and it came from the street outside. She sprang out of bed and looked out of the window. There was a large house across the road that belonged to a retired doctor, who was visiting relatives in Australia. Megan waited, not sure if she had dreamt it. She watched and waited for several minutes.

Everything seemed to be quiet. She was about to get back into bed, when she heard footsteps running in the street outside. She dashed to the window just in time to see the backs of two people dressed in black hooded jackets running down the street in the direction of Oakton Hall. They were carrying backpacks.

She wished she hadn't seen them. She didn't want to be a witness to a crime. Her dad would never cope with that. But then she told herself that she hadn't actually seen anything. The people she saw could have been returning home from a night out or something. She wasn't even sure if they were men or women and there may not have even been a crime at all. But some time later, as she was drifting into an uneasy sleep, a flashing blue light filled her bedroom. Someone had called the police.

The next day, Megan got up to the sound of her dad clattering dishes as he made breakfast. She was pleasantly surprised, because this was something he hadn't done for a long time. 'I've decided to go to the doctors,' he announced as they ate their toast and jam. 'Bill talked me into it yesterday.'

Megan looked anxious. This was her biggest fear. If the doctor found out that her dad was too ill to look after her, she may have to go into care.

'It's not fair on you when I'm so tired and can't do anything,' he said quietly. 'I'll see if I can get an appointment sometime this week.'

'Maybe you don't need to see a doctor,' said Megan quickly. 'You made breakfast this morning. I think you're getting better.'

'No, I'm not getting better,' said Paul raising his voice. 'It's no good pretending I'm alright, because you know very well I'm not!'

Megan knew how fragile her dad's moods were. Disagreeing with him now could send him back into his world of silence and she couldn't stand it anymore. 'OK,' she whispered meekly. 'That's fine.'

Paul sighed heavily and poured himself some more tea. 'You could go and see how Ryan is doing whilst I'm at the doctors,' he said. 'Then I won't have to worry about you being here on your own while I'm out.' Megan was pleased with this idea. There was so much she needed to talk to Ryan about. She just hoped that Bill would leave them alone for a while so they could talk in private.

It was the end of the week before Paul went to the doctors and Megan went round to Ryan's as arranged. A slim fair-haired woman in a smart navy-blue dress and high heels opened the door. Her voice was pleasant but high pitched. 'Oh hello. You must be Megan,' she said briskly. 'I'm Helena, Ryan's step-mum. Come in. Come in.'

She led Megan through to the lounge. Ryan was sitting on the settee with his leg propped up on a pillow, playing a game on his phone. He didn't have time to speak before Helena started talking again. 'I can't thank you enough for helping Ryan,' she said. 'I'm always telling him to take care, but he can be so clumsy. I think he's getting to those teenage years when he's growing so fast that his body can't keep up.'

Her laugh was even more high pitched than her speaking voice and she reminded Megan of a talkative parrot. She soon realised that there would be little chance of speaking to Ryan if Helena was around.

'Put that phone away Ryan,' snapped Helena, 'you've got a visitor. Would you like a drink Megan?' she carried on. 'I was just going to make some coffee. Do you drink coffee or would you rather have tea? Ryan would rather drink pop, but I'm always telling him that pop is bad for him and…'

'Tea will be fine. Thank you,' Megan interrupted.

Ryan seemed as relieved as she was when Helena finally left the room. 'She'll be going back to work soon,' he muttered. 'She's just waiting for Bill to come back. He's taken Skippy for a walk.' Megan dropped her voice. 'Do you know if there've been any more burglaries?'

'Yeah. Grandad told me the house across the road was broken into earlier this week. What are you whispering for?'

Megan moved to a chair facing the door, so she could stop talking when Helena came back in. 'I haven't told anyone, but I heard glass smashing the other night and I saw two people with backpacks running down the road.'

Ryan lowered his voice. 'Could one of them have been Kirsty?'

'Would you two like some biscuits?' called Helena from the kitchen.

'Yes please.' they chorused.

Megan was annoyed at Ryan's suggestion. 'I don't know why you suspect Kirsty. We've no proof she's involved.'

Ryan leaned forward. 'We can't prove it, but I've been thinking about it. Everything points to it being her.'

'Like what?' said Megan.

'She could easily climb in through a smashed window, then stash the stolen stuff in that huge bag of hers and run off,' said Ryan excitedly. 'Have you noticed how she's always running near the watchtower? I bet she's hiding the stolen goods in there. She works at the Hall so she could easily have stolen the key.' He sat back with a sense of satisfaction, but Megan was becoming irritated. 'That's all just coincidence,' she said. 'You just don't like her for some reason.'

'Help yourself to these,' said Helena cheerfully as she placed a plate of biscuits on the coffee table and disappeared back into the kitchen.

Ryan glanced at the door to make sure Helena had gone before he carried on. 'Kirsty's too good to be true with all that cheerfulness. It's all put on. I know it is. She's just like Helena.'

'That doesn't make her a thief though does it,' replied Megan. 'And she certainly wasn't cheerful when you fell. She was panicking then.'

'Did you see the way she hugged Skippy when we got to the bench?' said Ryan.

'I mean, I love dogs, but that was seriously weird.' He waved his hand towards the biscuits. 'Pass me a chocolate one will you, Megan? I can't get up.'

Megan suddenly felt bad that she hadn't asked Ryan how he was feeling, but he seemed OK as he munched on his biscuit.

'Your dad looked so mad when we came back with Irene,' said Ryan. 'What did he say?'

There was a loud bark as the front door opened and Skippy scampered in, followed by Bill. When Helena eventually announced she was going back to work, it took her a long time to leave. She fussed over Ryan and even brought him a blanket, as if he were a young child. Megan noticed that Ryan became surly when Helena was around and he hardly responded when she spoke to him. Bill was also becoming agitated.

'You need to buy a better lock for your shed Bill,' said Helena as she put on her coat. 'With all these burglaries happening round here, you can't be too careful. You've got some valuable car parts in there.'

Bill growled a response. 'OK. I'll get a new lock next week.'

'Next week might be too late,' said Helena, pulling her car keys from the depths of her handbag. 'Oh, and by the way,' she added, 'You need to get some more bread. There's none left in the freezer.'

You could almost hear the sigh of relief from everyone when Helena finally left.

Bill rolled his eyes in frustration. 'I'd better go and buy some bread then, hadn't I?' he said. 'I won't be long.'

Megan was thankful for some time to talk to Ryan alone. She wanted to tell him what she had found out. 'My dad was all worked up when I got back,' said Megan, 'but he calmed down after a bit, so I was able to ask him about the car crash.'

'What did he tell you?' asked Ryan.

'He wouldn't say much,' said Megan, 'but he said it happened just after my seventh birthday, even though he once told me it happened when I was six.'

'That's a bit strange,' said Ryan. 'Did he tell you where it happened?'

'Not exactly,' said Megan. 'He just said it was somewhere off the York Road, but I already knew that.'

Ryan was becoming more intrigued. 'Did you ask him what caused it?'

'The car she was driving hit a tree,' explained Megan. 'Dad thinks she was distracted by something, because there was nothing wrong with her or the car and there were no other cars involved.'

'Well at least you know now anyway,' said Ryan trying to sound comforting.

'But there are still things I don't understand!' exclaimed Megan.

'Like what?'.

'Like where I was when the car crashed.'

Ryan was puzzled. 'Why is that important?'

Megan tried to explain. 'My birthday's at the beginning of August. If it happened just after my birthday, then it would be the summer holidays. I wouldn't be at school during the holidays, so where was I?'

Ryan was thoughtful. 'Maybe your dad was looking after you,' he suggested, 'or you were with a child-minder.'

Megan shook her head. 'No, there's more to it than that. I know there is. My dad was very secretive when I asked him for more details. He said there's no point filling my head with memories that will haunt me. Well how can I have memories of the crash if I wasn't even there?'

Ryan bit his lip. 'Megan,' he said cautiously, 'I've just thought of something.'

'What?'

'Do you think you could have been in the car when it crashed?' he said softly. 'You could have blotted it out of your memory. That can happen you know. I once saw a programme about it.'

Megan's face drained of colour. 'If I was in the car, I could have been the one who distracted her. Maybe that's why no-one will tell me what happened.'

Ryan and Megan were so deep in thought that they didn't notice Skippy as she wandered over to the biscuits on the table. All they heard was a loud snap as she gobbled one of the biscuits, sending the plate flying to the floor. 'Skippy!' they both shouted at once. But Skippy had run off into the kitchen to hide. It made them both laugh. Megan picked up the biscuits from the floor and carried them into the kitchen. Skippy, who was under the table, looked longingly at the rest of the biscuits. Her soft appealing eyes were nothing like the harsh golden eyes of the wild cat. Megan smiled. She took a couple of biscuits from the plate and threw them to Skippy, before putting the rest in the bin. Skippy had been a distraction, but the thought that she might be to blame for her mother's death caused a pain in her heart that just wouldn't go away. She had to find someone who would tell her the truth, no matter how painful it would be.

Bill's phone was in the kitchen and next to it was a little book of telephone numbers. It crossed Megan's mind that if Bill knew Irene's late husband, he might still have their phone number in his phone book, and she was right. She looked around for a pen, tore a piece of paper from a nearby pad and copied down the number.

'You OK Megan?' Ryan called.

'I've found Irene's number in Bill's phone book,' she said, as she came back into the lounge. 'I'm going to call her. I want to see if I can persuade her to tell me what she knows, but I don't know when I can do it. We only have a landline and my dad hardly ever leaves me in the house on my own.'

Ryan put his hand in his pocket and pulled out his phone. 'You can call her on this.'

Megan hesitated. 'I need to think about it first. I'm not sure what to say.'

'Just ask her if you were in the car when it crashed,' said Ryan.

Megan began to have second thoughts. 'Maybe it's not such a good idea to phone,' she said. 'I might get too upset, but I could write her a letter explaining how important it is for me to know the truth. I know her address.'

'Have you ever asked my Grandad about the crash?' asked Ryan. 'He must know something about what happened.'

'I did ask him once,' said Megan. 'It was some time ago. He got really upset and told me to ask my dad, so I never mentioned it again.'

'What makes you think Irene will tell you anything?' said Ryan.

'She told me she would try to persuade Bill to go and see my dad,' said Megan. 'She was my mum's best friend and I think deep down she really wants to help me.'

Ryan sighed in frustration. 'Why won't your dad talk to you about things? Is there something wrong with him?'

But before Megan had a chance to answer, there was a knock at the door.

'Grandad's forgotten his keys again,' said Ryan.

Megan looked out of the window. 'It's not your grandad.' she cried in amazement. 'It's Kirsty!'

'What does *she* want?' grumbled Ryan. 'Don't answer the door.'

'It's too late. She's seen me,' said Megan. She bundled the barking Skippy into the kitchen and opened the door.

'Megan,' said Kirsty effusively, 'I didn't expect to see you here. I've come to see how Ryan is.' She waved a box of chocolates in front of Megan as she stepped into the house. 'I thought these might cheer him up,' she grinned.

Ryan's face was glum. 'Thanks,' he muttered grudgingly as Kirsty handed him the chocolates. 'How did you know where I lived?'

Kirsty winked at Megan and spoke in a mock sinister tone. 'Ah! I have ways of finding things out,' she joked.

'I bet you have!' replied Ryan knowingly. 'I bet you know all about everyone round here and what houses they live in as well.'

'I see you aren't any more cheerful,' said Kirsty pulling a face. 'Is your ankle still painful?'

Ryan's continued rudeness was making Megan feel uncomfortable. He seemed to be ignoring Kirsty's question so she answered for him. 'It's a bad sprain not a break and it's much better than it was, isn't it Ryan?'

'I know it's just a sprain,' replied Kirsty, 'Irene told me.'

Megan was surprised. 'I didn't know you were a friend of Irene's.'

'I didn't know her before I met you,' she replied. 'I happened to see her when I ran past the gatehouses this morning. She was just going out in her car.'

'So that's how you know where I live,' mumbled Ryan.

Kirsty waved both her hands in the air. 'Hurray! He's talking to me at last!' she mocked.

Ryan sat back and glared at Kirsty as she sat down in Bill's chair. They could hear Skippy still barking in the kitchen. 'You can let Skippy in here if you like,' said Kirsty. 'Was she OK after the fire?'

'She was fine,' answered Ryan coldly. 'It was good of you to cuddle her so much. You must love dogs as much as people.'

'Do you have a dog of your own?' asked Megan, trying to be more friendly.

'Sadly no,' answered Kirsty, 'but I used to help out at a dog's home, when I was younger.'

Ryan didn't say anything, but when she stood up to look into Bill's glass display cabinet, he watched her suspiciously.

'Nice antiques in here,' she remarked. 'Your grandad has some interesting things.'

She picked up a photo of Skippy from on top of the cabinet. 'I know who this is,' she said.

Ryan was angry. 'All Bill's things are very precious to him,' he said, 'and if anyone were to steal them it would break his heart.'

Kirsty was either unaware of Ryan's feelings towards her or she pretended not to care.

'Yes, that would be terrible,' she agreed. 'Well, I'd better be going. I've some more running to do yet and I've got to take my car into Ray's Garage. One of my tyres is losing air.'

Ryan remembered that she started to deny she had a two-seater sports car when they were in the woods, but he was convinced she was lying. 'Do you need special tyres for that sports car?' he asked casually.

Kirsty looked slightly annoyed. 'I haven't got a sports car. I don't know where you got that idea from Ryan. I only have a second-hand Mini.'

Megan tried to explain. 'You said you had a new red car, so when we saw a red Sprite in the car park at Oakton Hall the other day, we thought it was yours.'

Kirsty laughed. 'I think I know the car you mean. I only wish it were mine, but that's Sarah's. You know her Megan, it's Joe's wife. She works on reception at the Hall.'

'How can she afford a classic sports car on a receptionist's wages?' asked Ryan, cynically.

'Her dad owns Ray's Garage in York,' explained Kirsty. 'He's a classic car dealer. He lets her drive the cars to work now and again. Anyway, what time is it? I've got to go.' It was when she rolled up her sleeve to look at her watch, that Megan saw the scars on her arm and hand. She had noticed them before in the swimming pool and she wondered how Kirsty had got them.

Bill arrived back just as Kirsty was leaving. 'I didn't know you had so many admirers Ryan,' he said, as Kirsty drove away. Ryan quickly changed the subject. 'Grandad, did you once tell me you used to work at Ray's Garage in York?'

Bill was surprised. 'Yes, I worked there for many years. Why?'

'Ray's daughter Sarah works at the Hall,' said Ryan coolly. 'Does Ray have classic cars?'

Bill was always delighted to talk about cars. 'Yes. I used to work on them. Mostly sports cars. I became quite an expert on them in the end,' he said proudly.

'We saw one in the car park at the Hall,' said Ryan. 'Kirsty said Sarah had driven it there.'

'Quite possibly,' said Bill smiling. 'Sarah was always interested in driving the sports cars, but not so keen on cleaning them,' he chuckled. 'She didn't want to spoil her nails. Mind you, Ray has two youths running a car wash there now I believe. They were down by the shops yesterday posting leaflets through doors.'

Bill's eyes glazed over as he started to recall his working days with fondness. 'Your dad used to come with me to the garage when he was younger Ryan,' he said warmly, 'and Paul used to come too sometimes,' he said turning to Megan. 'The things they used to get up to when I wasn't looking …'

'Does Ray have one of those Sprites with headlights on the bonnet, Grandad?' said Ryan. 'What did you call it Megan?'

'A Frog-Eyed Sprite,' said Megan.

Bill didn't answer straight away. He looked anxious. 'Yes, he still has a couple of those I think,' he mumbled. 'I'll go and make some tea.'

Ryan was shocked. He had never known his grandad become suddenly silent like this before and he couldn't help but wonder why.

There was a tap at the window. Paul had returned from the doctors and Megan went to let him in.

A few seconds later, Paul put his head round the door. To Megan's surprise he sounded quite calm. 'Glad you're on the mend Ryan,' he said. 'Give my regards to your dad when you see him. We were at school together you know.'

When Bill came back into the lounge after Megan and her dad had left, he was carrying the local newspaper. 'Paul's just given me this to read,' he said pointing to a short paragraph on an inside page.

'What is it?' asked Ryan.

Bill handed the paper to Ryan. 'Read it to me will you Ryan, I can't find my glasses.'

Ryan took the paper from Bill and read it aloud.

BURGLARS STEAL FAMILY WAR MEDALS

First World War medals belonging to a brave soldier who served in the army were stolen from a house in Lakeside Close, Oakton on February 2nd. The medals belonged to the late grandfather of a 70-year-old woman. The burglars also stole some jewellery including her grandmother's engagement ring. Detective Constable

Sharon Rowlands of the local CID said, 'The medals and the ring are of great sentimental value to the victim and are irreplaceable.' Anyone with any information is asked to contact 101.

Bill sighed. 'Poor Mary,' he said softly as he sat down in his chair.

'Whoever stole those things must have hearts of stone.'

7

The Special Envelope

Dear Irene. Megan put down her pen for the third time that night. She just couldn't think what to write. In fact, that wasn't the only thing she couldn't do. All she could think about was finding out if she was to blame for what happened to her mother. The idea tormented her to such an extent that she couldn't face getting up the next day. All she wanted to do was lie on her bed and hide under the duvet. When her dad came into her room to see what was wrong, she told him she wasn't feeling well. He looked annoyed.

'That's all I need,' he said abruptly. 'I've got enough to worry about without you being sick.'

Megan couldn't believe he was so unsympathetic. 'I can't help feeling ill Dad,' she said angrily, 'and anyway, what exactly have you got to worry about?'

'I wasn't going to tell you, but I'm going for some tests soon,' he replied.

Megan began to feel scared. 'What kind of tests?'

'The doctor wants to check there's nothing physically wrong with me before she sends me to see one of those counsellors,' said Paul quietly.

Megan had once seen someone called a counsellor when she was much younger. A woman had come to the house a few times to help her make her memory box, just after her mum died and it had made her feel a little better. But the thought of her dad getting worse upset her and she was terrified of going into care. 'You're not very ill though Dad, are you?' she said hopefully. 'I'm sure they'll sort it out soon.'

But Paul didn't answer. To Megan's horror, he put his head in his hands and began to cry like a baby. She didn't know what to do. This wasn't the first time her dad had broken down in front of her, but it was still a shock. 'It's OK Dad,' she said gently. 'I'm sorry I'm a worry to you. I'll be fine.'

She wanted to help him, but she also felt angry. This was not how it was meant to be. A father should be the one looking after his daughter, not the other way round. Her mind flashed back to a time when she was very young. Her dad had taken her to a park and she had hurt her leg falling off a swing. She remembered how he had comforted her and how he carried her all the way home, singing silly songs to make her feel better. She watched helplessly as Paul dabbed his weary eyes. When he looked at her, he didn't seem like the same dad any more. It seemed like he was empty inside.

Megan continued to be worried. She didn't feel like eating and she didn't sleep much either. On the day before she was due to go back to school after the half-term break, her dad decided to make some beans on toast for them both. As they sat at the table, Paul watched her as she pushed the beans around the plate with her fork.

'For goodness sake Megan either eat the food or leave it alone,' he snapped.

'I told you I wasn't hungry,' she answered.

'I know you said you weren't feeling very well,' said Paul a little more kindly, 'but is there something worrying you? Is that why you're not eating?'

Megan was surprised. Her dad rarely noticed how she was feeling these days. She took a deep breath. Now was her chance to ask him about the crash. *After all,* she thought to herself, *things can't get much worse.*

'Dad,' she said firmly. 'Was I in the car when mum crashed?'

Paul looked astonished. 'Whatever gave you that idea?'

'Just tell me Dad,' she pleaded.

'I'm telling you now Megan,' replied Paul slowly. 'You were not, most definitely not in the car and that's the truth.'

When Megan looked into her dad's eyes, she believed him. But there were now more questions to ask. 'If I wasn't in the car, then where was I? I was only just seven and it was the summer holidays, so why wasn't I with my mum?' She was shaking now. The lack of food and sleep was having an effect.

Paul looked upset by Megan's question. She was convinced he was going to shout at her like he usually did, but to her surprise he just sighed impatiently and when he spoke there was a deep bitterness in his voice. 'Someone else was looking after you,' he said. 'And before you ask who that person was,' he continued, 'I will tell you. It was that woman, Irene Croft! She was the one who was supposed to be looking after you while your mother went to York.'

Megan was shocked at his reply. 'What do you mean *supposed* to be looking after me?'

Paul stood up and kicked his chair away from the table with such force that it fell over and crashed to the floor. 'Now look what you've made me do,' he bellowed, picking up the chair. 'Why are you pushing me into telling you things Megan?' he shouted. 'I'm not ready for it.'

'Please Dad, don't get upset,' she pleaded. 'I just want to know a few more small details that's all.'

Paul ignored her and stormed into the lounge. There was a time when such an incident would have sent her crying to her room, but this time Megan decided to follow him. However, when she stood up she felt strange. The room seemed to be swirling round. She gripped the edge of the kitchen table and heaved herself up. This time she would not give up her efforts to find out the truth. She braced herself as she took a deep breath and stumbled towards the lounge.

Paul didn't look up when Megan came in. He was slumped in his chair staring at the floor. She steadied herself on the arm of the settee and sat down shakily. She knew she had to be brave. She knew she had to keep up the pressure on her dad, but she just wished she didn't feel so strange. 'I already know some things Dad,' she said weakly, 'and I'm starting to remember other things myself.'

Paul sat upright in his chair. He looked alarmed. 'What sort of things are you talking about?' he said. 'What exactly do you remember about the crash?'

What little colour Megan had in her cheeks suddenly drained away, as she realised what her dad was trying to say. She let out a gasp as if she couldn't get her breath.

'What do you mean "*What do I remember?*"' she cried. 'Did I see it happen? Was I there?'

The next thing Megan knew she was lying on the settee with her eyes closed. She thought she could hear a woman calling her name again. She thought she was in the woods. She was hiding, but it was just a game. It was a game of hide and seek. 'Megan! Megan!' she heard again. But this time it was her dad's voice.

'You've fainted Megan,' said her dad trying his best to keep calm. 'You'll be OK when you've had something to eat and drink. Sit up and I'll get you some water.'

As Megan began to gather her thoughts, she knew it was no good asking her dad for any more information. She had spoilt it by fainting. She was angry with herself for being so weak, but the game of hide and seek in the woods was worrying her. Who was the woman calling her name? Was it

Irene or was it someone else? This was the second time she'd had this memory. Was she remembering something that really happened, or was it just her mind playing tricks on her?

'Don't ask me any more about the crash Megan,' said Paul sternly as he passed her some water. 'You're making us both ill with your constant questions. I will decide when you're old enough to be told everything and it's not now.'

As Megan sipped her water she realised just how much she needed to talk to Irene. If Irene was looking after her when her mother went to York, she was bound to know something about that day.

Later that night, Megan sat in her room and took out her pen once more. *Dear Irene,* she wrote. *Please help me find the truth…* The words came more easily now. First, she wrote down everything her dad had told her and then she wrote down everything she still wanted to know. She asked Irene if anyone actually saw the crash and asked her why everyone was being so secretive about it. She realised that if Irene sent a letter back to her, there was a risk her dad would open it. So she told Irene she would call at the gatehouse with Ryan when he was better. She explained that she would have to go with Ryan, because her dad would never let her go out alone.

The next morning, whilst her dad was having a shave, she took a stamp and an envelope from the drawer in the kitchen and took it back upstairs to write the address. Then she put the letter in her school bag and posted it on her way to school. All she had to do now was wait for Ryan's ankle to get better.

A week later, when Megan called to see Ryan after school, it was obvious that something had happened. He couldn't wait for Bill to go into the kitchen, so he could speak to Megan alone. 'Irene's coming here on Sunday,' he said excitedly. 'You need to come round when she's here Megan, but don't tell your dad she's coming.'

Megan's mind was racing. This was an opportunity not to be missed, but she couldn't just arrive and start talking about her mum. Then she had an idea.

'I've got a photo of Bill and my mum taken outside my house,' said Megan. 'I could bring that round to start the conversation.'

'Great idea,' answered Ryan. 'She's coming early on Sunday afternoon.'

There was no more time to talk as Bill came back in the room and so it wasn't long before Megan made her excuses and left.

She was grateful that her dad was watching TV when she got home, because she needed to look for the photo. She was hoping it was among the many photos of her mother that she kept in her memory box. Some time ago, her dad had gathered up all the old photo albums and the photos of her mum in frames and put them away in the loft. So, if the photo wasn't in her box, she knew she would not be able to get it.

After closing her bedroom door, she reached for the memory box on the bedside table. It was decorated with pictures of colourful flowers and had the words 'Megan's Memory Box' written on the lid in her old childish handwriting. The photos were wrapped up in a paper bag tied up with a white ribbon. She carefully undid the ribbon and took the precious photos out of the bag one by one, laying each one on the bed as she did so. She hadn't looked at them for some time. She was always worried that her dad might come into her room when she was looking at them and get upset. If he came in now, she would just have to face the consequences.

It wasn't long before she found the photo she was looking for. Bill and her mum were standing outside her house, next to a blue Mini car with a white stripe down the bonnet. Her mother was dressed in a brightly coloured printed top with a string of dark green beads round her neck that set off her long red curly hair. Megan thought about all the days she had spent without her mother and before she knew it, a large tear dropped onto the photo. She wiped it off impatiently with her finger. There was no time for such sorrow. She had to focus on how to get the photo out of the house without her dad noticing. She took a closer look at it. Just in the corner she could make out a child's hand on the gatepost. She guessed the hand must be hers. She assumed her dad must have taken the photo and that the car was one of the Minis he used to own. She hid the photo inside her homework book and started to make her plan.

The only coat with pockets large enough to hide the photo was the white padded coat that she hated so much. It was now hanging back on the hook in the hallway. Her dad often stood by the door and watched her whenever she went out, so she would need to put the photo in the pocket some time before she left. She planned to do it when he was having a shower the next morning.

For once, everything went according to plan and on Sunday afternoon Megan set off to Ryan's house wearing her padded coat with the photo safely hidden in one of the pockets. Thankfully, her dad was so pleased she was wearing her coat again, that he didn't question why she needed to wear it just to go next door. When Megan arrived, Irene was already there. She could see by Irene's face that she was surprised. Bill was on edge and quickly darted into the kitchen to get the cakes he had bought specially for Irene's visit.

"How's Zoe?' asked Ryan, in an effort to break the ice.

Irene seemed relieved to be talking about the cat. 'She's a lot better thank you. She even seems to be putting on weight,' she added. 'Probably too much weight.'

'A bit like me,' said Bill, as he appeared with the plate of cakes. 'I didn't know you still had Mike's cats Irene. I thought you were going to give them away.'

'Yes, well... he wanted to breed them,' said Irene nervously, 'so I decided to keep them. They're no trouble really.'

'I never actually saw them,' said Bill as he offered round the cakes. 'Mike was very secretive about them. He said they were from Scotland and worth a lot of money.'

Bill paused as he patted Skippy who had come in looking for tasty snacks. 'I prefer dogs myself.'

As Irene fidgeted in her chair, Megan and Ryan began to realise that everyone, including Bill, thought Irene's cats were just ordinary cats. Luckily for Irene, Bill didn't ask any more questions about the cats and the conversation moved on to talking about the burglaries. Ryan gave Megan a knowing look as she sat nervously, twisting the ends of her red pony tail around her fingers. He wondered if she was ever going to bring out the photo. But Megan was biding her time. She was waiting for the right moment. So, when Bill started to talk about the old days and the cars he used to repair for Irene's late husband, she knew that the right moment had come. 'Oh, I've got something to show you,' she said, trying to appear casual. 'It's in my coat pocket.'

Hoping they wouldn't notice her trembling hands, she placed the photo on the table. Then she sat back and waited. Bill was the first to speak. 'Oh yes I remember that day,' he said warmly. 'Your mum had just taken delivery of your dad's latest Mini. He had a few Minis in his time, but that one was the worst. Maggie was the one who drove it the most and it was always breaking down. She had to keep ringing Ray to come and fix it.'

'Why didn't my dad drive it?' asked Megan.

'He drove it at weekends,' said Bill, 'but he also had a van for his electrical business. He was out in the van when the Mini arrived.'

Megan was surprised. 'Who took the photo then, if it wasn't my dad?'

Bill looked up from the photo and glanced at Irene. It was a strange, lingering glance full of unspoken meaning. 'It was me,' said Irene quietly. 'I took it.'

Megan had a feeling that she was on the cusp of a wave of truth that was just about to tumble out. She knew that the next question she asked would be crucial. She took a deep breath to calm herself and then looked directly at Irene. 'Did you spend much time with my mum?' she asked. 'Only I just wondered what she was like.' She wanted to hear from Irene, but it was Bill who answered.

'She was a lovely person and that's all you need to know really isn't it?' he said reassuringly. Megan felt frustrated. 'No, it isn't,' she said quickly. 'I want to know what she was like. I mean what sort of person was she?' Irene's reply was unexpected. 'She was a bit eccentric. A bit on the wild side. Wouldn't you agree Bill?'

'I suppose you could say that,' laughed Bill.

Ryan was intrigued. 'What do you mean wild?' he asked.

Irene began to relax and sat back in her chair before she replied. 'Maggie was a very determined person,' she declared. 'She would get an idea in her head and that was it.'

Bill also looked less tense. 'Do you remember when she painted all the woodwork in her house bright pink?' he chuckled.

'Oh yes,' smiled Irene. 'Paul made her repaint it the next day.'

'She used to paint pictures as well, didn't she?' said Bill. 'She painted some lovely portraits.'

Irene nodded. 'Yes, she was due to start a course at York Art College just before she...' her voice trailed off, but Bill carried on. 'Do you remember the day she went on a charity run and got lost? I mean how can you get lost on an organised run, but she did. She tried to take a short cut across some fields and ended up walking even further to get back.'

By now Bill was laughing so heartily that his eyes were watering. Dabbing his eyes with a tissue, his memories of Maggie seemed to be unstoppable. How Megan wished she'd had enough courage to ask him about her mum before.

'What about the day Maggie sprayed the inside of that blue Mini with a really strong perfume,' he laughed.

'I do remember that,' smiled Irene. 'She gave me a lift to York and the smell made me feel sick.'

It was the mention of the Mini again that gave Megan the opening she had been waiting for. 'Was she driving that blue Mini when she had the crash?' she asked tentatively.

With this one short question, the mood in the room darkened and Bill's face changed.

'No,' he muttered almost inaudibly. 'She wasn't.'

Irene looked at Bill. 'Paul needs to tell her,' she said earnestly. 'It's not fair on any of us, least of all Megan.'

Bill sighed. 'It's your dad that needs to tell you what happened,' he said softly. 'I'll have a word with him tomorrow.'

'No,' said Irene sharply. 'You're putting it off Bill. You need to go tonight. Maggie wouldn't want Megan to suffer like this would she? I would go and see him myself, but you know how he feels about me.'

'OK, OK,' said Bill irritably. 'I'll go tonight.'

Megan couldn't say any more. She just swallowed hard. The torrent of tears waiting behind her eyes was dangerously close to spilling over.

That night, after Megan had gone to bed, there was a knock at the front door. She could hear Bill's voice as Paul greeted him and then she heard the lounge door closing behind them. She ran to the top of the stairs, but all she could hear were muffled voices. She was disappointed that she couldn't hear what was being said, but at least Bill had kept his promise.

From where she was standing she could see into her dad's bedroom. She glanced aimlessly at the usual mess of papers on the floor but as she did so, her eyes caught sight of a large box on top of his wardrobe. Her dad had once told her that it contained important papers and warned her not to touch it. But now things were different. There could be things in that box that might give her more information about her mother.

Thinking that Bill and her dad would be talking for a while, she crept into her dad's room and looked for something to stand on to reach the box. There was a wooden chair next to his bed with clothes thrown over it. She lifted all the clothes onto the bed and placed the chair in front of the wardrobe. She was only small, but when she stood on the chair, she could just reach the box. Grasping it with both hands, she climbed off the chair and placed the box on the floor. It was covered in dust. She lifted the hinged lid with the tips of her fingers and slowly opened the box. Inside was a large sketch book with the initials MT on the cover and a large brown envelope. She wondered if this was what it felt like to break into someone's house to steal something.

She was about to open the envelope when the sound of her dad's raised voice made her jump. The lounge door opened and then the front door slammed. It sounded like there had been an argument and Bill had left. She put the envelope on the bed. There was no time to look at the sketch book, so she left it in the box. As she quickly climbed onto the chair to put the box back, it slipped from her hands, landing on the floor with a thud. 'Megan,' called Paul from downstairs. 'What are you doing?'

'I'm fine Dad,' she called back. 'Just reading and dropped my book that's all.'

Picking up the box again, she returned it to the top of the wardrobe and gently climbed off the chair. With shaking hands, she lifted up the chair to put it back by the bed, but as she did so, one of the chair legs caught the bedroom door with a sharp bang. Her dad's angry voice bellowed at her from the bottom of the stairs yet again. 'What are you doing now Megan? Get to bed!'

Snatching up the envelope, she raced out of the bedroom. 'Sorry Dad. I'm just going to the bathroom.'

There was no response. Paul went back into the lounge and slammed the door. Megan listened and waited. She could hear nothing apart from the pounding of her heart as she stood motionless in the bathroom with the envelope still in her hand.

A few minutes later she was back in her bedroom, looking for a place to hide it. There was only one place her dad would never look and that was in her memory box.

She turned the envelope over and over in her hands. Something felt wrong. Some-how she just couldn't bring herself to open it. She felt guilty for taking it and she was terrified at the thought of what she might or might not discover. A cold chill rippled through her body. Clutching the envelope tightly to her chest, she pulled back the duvet and slid into the warmth of her comforting bed. She lay there for a few moments with her head on the pillow, cradling the envelope against her body like a baby with a soft toy. She wondered if she ought to put the envelope back where she found it. Everyone seemed to be saying she was too young to know the truth and perhaps they were right. Maybe it was too horrible to face up to. Then without warning, warm tears flowed onto her pillow as if from nowhere, making her hold the envelope that little bit tighter. Then she knew that she couldn't put it back. She had come too far in her search for the truth to give up now. Whatever was in the envelope, it couldn't be worse than not knowing.

8

A Newspaper Cutting

She woke up with a start and looked at the clock. It was 1 a.m. and the envelope was still in the bed. The light had been turned off, so her dad must have looked in and switched it off. She was thankful that the envelope was not on view. It then crossed her mind that this would be the best time to open it, as her dad would be asleep. It was too risky to put the light on, so she propped up her torch on the bed and gently pulled out some of the papers from the envelope. On the top was a folded paper that looked quite old. It was her mother's birth certificate. She held it closer to the torchlight, so it was easier to read. It said that her mother's name was Margaret Hawkins and that she was born in York. It also gave the names of her mother's parents – Susan and David Hawkins – and it gave her date of birth. She carefully put this to one side and unfolded another sheet which appeared to be her parents' marriage certificate. Inside the folded certificate was a photo of her mum and dad on their wedding day. Her mum looked beautiful, dressed in white. She was carrying a spray of bright red flowers that matched her red curly hair. The newlywed couple were standing in some gardens and looked really happy, but there was no family grouped around them. She had once asked her dad why she didn't have any grandparents and he told her they had all died. She had never heard him mention any aunts or uncles either. How she envied Ryan who had both his parents and his grandad still alive.

The torchlight flickered over the bed and she heard her dad coughing as he slept. Megan's eyes were hurting and she was desperately tired. She felt she needed more time to study what else was in the envelope, so she put it in her memory box and drifted into an uneasy sleep.

The next morning when Megan went downstairs to make her breakfast she heard someone putting something through the letter box. When she looked, there was another handwritten letter on the mat, addressed to her dad. She dashed to the front window and looked down the street, but whoever had posted the letter had gone. With everything that had been going on, she had forgotten to ask him about the last one and her dad had not mentioned it. This letter looked like the same handwriting. She wandered into the kitchen and put it on the table as she reached for an apple from the fruit bowl. She seemed to have permanently lost her appetite and couldn't face eating anything more.

She turned as Paul came into the kitchen. 'Someone's just posted another of those handwritten letters through the letterbox Dad,' she said as she bit into the apple. 'You didn't tell me who the last one was from.'

Paul snatched up the letter. 'Is that all you're having for breakfast?' he snapped. But he didn't wait for a reply before he continued. 'I don't want you going to Bill's house any more after school,' he stated bluntly. 'In fact, I don't want you going there at all,' he added.

Megan was astonished. 'But why?' she cried.

'You need to come home and do your homework,' he replied curtly. 'You'll never do well at school if you spend all your time round there. And don't bother arguing with me Megan because I've made up my mind.'

Before Megan could say any more, Paul stormed out of the

kitchen and marched up the stairs to his bedroom. There was no time to protest. Megan's school was in York and if she missed the next bus she would be late. When she left primary school, she had wanted to go to Oakton High School with her friends, but her dad said the one in York was a better school. He said there were too many rough kids at Oakton school, but Ryan went there and he seemed to be OK. If she was not at the same school as Ryan and not even allowed to visit him, she couldn't think how she was ever going to see Irene again. She just hoped that the envelope she had hidden in her memory box would tell her what else she needed to know.

As she sat on the school bus, she felt angry with her father and yet she was afraid to complain in case he got worse. Just like the wild cat in the watchtower, she felt completely alone and unable to break free.

When Megan returned from school that day, Paul was watching from the window. Two youths in hooded jackets were delivering leaflets across the street. 'I'm just watching those two,' he said as he opened the door. 'They're delivering leaflets about the car wash at Ray's Garage, but they seem to be taking their time. One of them has just stopped for a smoke. I hope they don't do that when they're cleaning cars.'

Megan didn't believe him. It was obvious he was standing there to make sure she didn't call on Ryan before she got home. She went into the house without saying a word. She could hardly bear to speak to him.

Later in the evening she decided to ask him again why she couldn't visit Ryan, but when he refused to even discuss it, she gave up and went to her room, saying she was going to do her homework.

After jamming a cushion behind her bedroom door to stop her dad coming in unexpectedly, she took the envelope out of her memory box and spread all the contents on the bed. She put the certificates to one side and then picked up a smaller white envelope containing a folded sheet of newspaper. From the condition of the newspaper she guessed it was published some time ago. As she carefully unfolded the page, a shocking headline came into view: *FATAL CAR CRASH IN OAKTON WOODS*. Her stomach churned when she saw the photo beneath the headline. The car that was crushed against a tree was some kind of sports car with the top down, but two other things caught her attention. In the background you could see Irene's gatehouse with a Mini parked outside. She couldn't tell what colour the Mini was because the newspaper photo was black and white, but it had a white stripe down the bonnet, just like the one in the photo of her mum and Bill. The newspaper report underneath the photo was quite factual and short. It gave her mother's name as the person who died and it said she was the driver of the sports car. It also mentioned that there were no other vehicles involved. But what stood out for Megan was the exact date and time of the crash. It was the afternoon of her seventh birthday. She felt stunned. She now realised why her dad didn't want to tell her exactly when her mum died. She felt guilty that she had been so angry with him, when he was only trying to ensure that her birthdays were free from sadness for as long as possible.

Then it occurred to her that whilst the discovery of this newspaper report answered the question about the date and time of the crash, it actually raised more questions. Why was her mother driving a sports car when the Mini was close by and why hadn't her dad told her that the car crashed by the gatehouses in Oakton woods? Then there was the question of where Megan was at the time of the crash. She worked out that if it happened outside Irene's house and Irene was looking after her, they both could have seen the crash or even caused it in some way. She also remembered her dad saying that her mum had gone to York on the day of the crash and she wondered what she had gone there for. Her mind was in a turmoil.

She took another look at the photograph of the crashed sports car. The more she looked at it, the more it looked like one of those Frog-Eyed Sprites. It certainly looked a lot like the one in the car park at Oakton Hall. She folded up the paper and put everything back in the envelope. She was glad she had seen the photo of the mangled car, but she didn't want to look at it ever again. It was just too painful.

As Megan lay in her bed that night, everything was going round in her head. Every time she found some answers there seemed to be more questions. Try as she might, she found it hard to remember much about being at Irene's house on her seventh birthday. Apart from a vague memory of playing hide and seek in the woods and playing with the knitted cats, she couldn't remember anything. She told herself that she would have to be patient. She would bide her time and wait for a chance to ask more questions. She was determined that she would never give up until she got what she wanted.

The next few weeks were very difficult. She couldn't seem to concentrate at school. She spent much of her time during lessons lost in thought as she invented different versions of what might have happened on her seventh birthday. Her teachers kept reminding her to pay attention, but thankfully the pupils in her class didn't notice anything different because they usually ignored her anyway. Being the only one in her year from the Oakton area meant that, right from her first day at the school, she felt like something of an outsider. The girls in her form seemed to have such different lives to her. They were allowed to go places at weekends and they had their own phones, which they constantly used to chat to each other every day. Some of them even had boyfriends. It was impossible for Megan to keep up with them and so in the end she stopped trying. During lunch breaks she would eat her lunch as fast as she could and then she would either go to the library or walk around the school trying to look as if she were going somewhere. In Megan's mind, anything was better than the shame of everyone knowing you had no friends to talk to. In fact, even though she could hardly call Ryan a friend, he was the only person she felt she could confide in and now she was not even allowed to see him.

At home things were also getting worse. Her dad was becoming more and more irritable. One evening after school Megan poured herself a glass of milk and accidentally knocked the glass over onto the kitchen floor. The splinting, crashing sound brought her dad scurrying in from the lounge. 'You stupid clumsy girl,' he shouted as he attempted to pick up the broken pieces of glass.

'Sorry Dad. I'll get a cloth…'

'No. Let me do it!' he yelled. 'You've done enough damage. Why can't you watch what you're doing? Just get out. Get out!'

Megan ran. She ran out of the kitchen and up the stairs to her room where she slammed the door shut and flung herself on her bed. The sense of injustice began to overwhelm her.

'Knocking over a glass of milk doesn't make me stupid,' she muttered to herself. 'It's not fair.' *Why did this happen to me?* she thought, as her eyes drifted to the memory box.

Why have I just got a memory box when everyone else has a mother? If my mum hadn't died I wouldn't need a stupid memory box. Seizing the box angrily with both hands, she raised it high in the air and threw it violently across the room. It landed with a crack as the lid flew open, spewing the precious contents over the floor like a stream of unwanted rubbish. She couldn't move.

She just sat on the bed and stared at the mess. She stared and stared as if she couldn't believe what she had done. There wasn't much in the box, but it was all she had left of her mother and she had tried to destroy it all.

Falling to her knees on the floor, she picked up the items one by one and put them carefully back in the box. Then she checked the catch, closed the lid and put it back on her bedside table, where it belonged. Only then did she cry. She knew no amount of crying would ever bring her mum back, but that night she cried because it felt like she had lost her dad as well.

Megan now spent most of her time in her bedroom when she got back from school, but sometimes she would sneak into her dad's room to see if she could see Ryan walking on crutches in the back garden. She once tried to attract his attention by knocking on her dad's bedroom window when she saw him, but her dad heard her and called her downstairs. She felt like a prisoner confined to a cell and sometimes she felt like she was suffocating.

Now and again, Paul made some attempts to make peace with Megan. He did a little housework and even offered to take her to York to buy a new coat, but she refused. She found it acutely embarrassing shopping for clothes with her father.

Things carried on in much the same way until a week later, when Megan was coming home from school on the bus. When it stopped opposite the local shop to pick up more passengers, she saw Ryan coming out carrying a newspaper. She knocked frantically on the bus window, but he got into Bill's car without noticing her and the bus drove away. She was bitterly disappointed, but at least she knew Ryan was now walking without his crutches. She got off the bus at the next stop and was just setting off towards her house when she heard someone calling her name. It was Joe. He was dressed in a track suit and was out of breath from running.

'I knew it was you Megan,' he said as he slowed down to walk beside her.

'I recognised your hair. It's just like your mother's. Has your dad read my letters yet?' he asked.

This comment took Megan completely by surprise, but before she could answer, they heard Kirsty calling them from across the road. Dressed in her usual running gear she ran over to join them. 'Hi,' she said brightly. 'Fancy seeing you two here.'

Joe looked uncomfortable. 'I've got to go,' he said quickly. 'Sarah finishes soon and I need to get to the Hall so I can get a lift home. See you later.'

Megan and Kirsty watched him as he ran off down the road. 'He won't tell me what he's training for,' said Kirsty. 'I think he's making it up. Are you OK Megan? You look lost in thought.'

Megan was still feeling shocked at the revelation that Joe had been sending letters to her dad and had also known her mum. On the spur of the moment she decided to see what Kirsty knew about Joe. 'I'm fine thanks,' said Megan brightly. 'I was just surprised to see Joe again that's all. I don't remember seeing him in Oakton before. Has he lived here long?'

'I think he's lived here for several years,' replied Kirsty as they walked along. 'He was in the army before he met Sarah. I think he was in the Far East or somewhere, but when he married Sarah he was out of work, so Ray gave him a job at his garage.'

'Why isn't he working there now then?' asked Megan.

'I'm not sure,' replied Kirsty, 'but I think something bad happened and Ray fired him. Sarah's been trying to find work for him ever since, but he has a nasty habit of getting fired from whatever job he ends up in.'

'Why's that?' asked Megan.

'He's got a quick temper, so they say,' said Kirsty. 'Although

I've always found him to be OK. Anyway,' she continued, 'never mind about Joe. How are you? We've not seen you at swimming club for a while. Is everything OK?'

Megan shrugged her shoulders. 'I've been busy,' she answered lamely.

Kirsty gave her a quizzical look but to Megan's relief she asked no more questions.

'I met Irene the other day,' said Kirsty. 'She's worried about one of her cats. It has a swollen stomach and won't eat.'

'Oh dear,' said Megan politely.

'I offered to take a look at it, but Irene said it doesn't like strangers,' said Kirsty.

Whilst Megan was pleased to see Kirsty, she was only half listening to what she was saying about the cat. She was wondering if there was any way that Kirsty could help her get in contact with Irene again.

'How's Ryan doing?' asked Kirsty suddenly.

'I don't know,' said Megan. 'I haven't seen him for a while.'

Kirsty looked concerned. 'How come?' she asked gently. 'I thought your dad and his grandad were close friends.'

Megan felt she had to tell Kirsty at least some part of the truth. 'My dad's had a row with Bill,' she explained, 'and I'm not allowed to go there anymore.'

As they got within sight of Megan's house, she could see her dad's face at the window, watching for her to come home. 'I can't talk any more,' said Megan. 'My dad wouldn't like it if he knew I'd told you that.'

Kirsty frowned. 'Megan,' she said softly, 'if you want to talk about anything, I'll be running past the bus stop at the same time tomorrow.' She then gave a friendly wave to Paul and carried on with her run.

Fortunately, Paul wasn't concerned when he saw Megan with Kirsty, because he knew who she was. He had met her some time ago when he took Megan for her first day at the swimming club. Megan remembered the embarrassment she felt when he told Kirsty to keep a close eye on his only daughter.

When Megan went to bed that night she had a bit of a headache. She kept wondering about what could be in Joe's letters and fretting about whether or not to ask her dad about them. When she finally looked at the clock by her bed, it was after midnight. Having decided that a drink of milk might help her sleep, she stumbled to the top of the stairs. Her dad's bedroom door was open and his bed was empty. There was a light on in the lounge, so she guessed he was still there. 'Just getting some milk Dad,' she called as she passed the lounge door. But there was no reply. She guessed her dad was in one of his quiet moods again, so she made her way into the kitchen, poured herself some milk and went back to bed.

It was her alarm clock that woke her next morning. She turned it off roughly. Her head was still aching. The last thing she felt like was going to school, but she thought school would probably be better than a day at home with her dad if he was in one of his silent moods. She threw off the duvet and made her way to the bathroom. Out of the corner of her half-closed eyes she noticed that her dad's door was still open and his bed hadn't been slept in. She ran down the stairs. 'Dad,' she called 'Where are you?'

As she pushed open the door of the lounge, she knew something was wrong, because the light was still on. Her dad was lying curled up on the settee. His eyes were closed and there was an empty bottle of whisky on the floor beside his head. She shook him by the shoulder. 'Dad, wake up. Wake up!' Her mind was racing with unimaginable thoughts. *What if he won't wake up?* She shook him again, but his eyes stayed shut and his body was limp. 'Dad! Dad!' she screamed. 'It's me Megan. Open your eyes. Say something.'

'What?' he grunted, opening his eyes blearily. 'What's happening?'

'You've been here all night,' said Megan tearfully.

Paul held on to the back of the settee with one hand and slowly pulled himself up to a sitting position. He put his head in his hands.

'Can you get me some water Megan?' he asked huskily. 'And turn out that light will you. It's hurting my eyes.'

When Megan came back with the water, Paul was still sitting with his head in his hands. He took the water and sipped it before handing it back to Megan. She placed it on the table, along with the empty whisky bottle from the floor.

'I'm so sorry Megan,' said Paul. 'I'm such a useless father. I'm just a waste of space. I can't seem to get my head right.'

Megan sat beside him. He reached out and gently took hold of her hand, just as he had done when she was little. 'I do love you Megan,' he whispered. 'Whatever happens, I love you more than anything. I want you to know that.'

She held his hand tightly. 'It's OK Dad. I know.'

'I can't look after you any more love,' he said quietly. 'I'm a bad father. You deserve better than this.'

'I'm OK Dad. I can look after myself,' said Megan quickly.

'But you're only twelve. You shouldn't have to look after yourself and you shouldn't have to look after me either.'

Megan was now beginning to panic. She didn't want to hear her dad talking like this.

'It's fine Dad, I don't mind,' said Megan.

'Someone else needs to look after you until I'm better,' said Paul suddenly.

Megan's face went pale. 'There is no one who can do that Dad. I'm OK. I am really.'

Paul sighed heavily. 'There are people who foster children

when their parents are ill Megan. You would be properly looked after there.'

Megan let go of her dad's hand as the tears began to stream down her face. 'No Dad. I want to stay with you. We'll manage. I don't want to go anywhere else.'

Paul put his arms around Megan. 'I don't really want you to go, but I feel so useless. I want to do what's best for you that's all.'

'What's best for me is to stay with you Dad,' sobbed Megan. 'We can work it out together. I know we can.'

Paul brushed away a tear from the corner of his eye. 'I don't deserve to have such a lovely daughter.'

Megan wiped her tear-stained face and passed her dad the box of tissues. 'Do you want some black coffee?' she asked.

Paul tried his best to smile. 'That's exactly what I need,' he said, 'but you don't look too good yourself Megan. Are you alright?'

'I've got a headache,' said Megan.

'Pass me the phone,' said Paul. 'I'll ring the school. I think we both need to stay at home and get some rest today.'

Paul went back to bed after drinking his coffee and it wasn't long before Megan decided to do the same. But she wasn't in bed long before she started to feel much worse. She had a high temperature and felt sick. When Paul got up around midday, he warmed up some soup and brought it to her room in a big mug. She struggled to drink it, but she felt thankful that her dad was making an effort to cope. That night her dad gave her some pain killers to help lower her temperature, but she was no better in the morning.

'You'd better stay in bed again today Megan,' he said gently. 'I'll ring the school and then I'll cancel my appointment at the doctor's.'

Megan forced herself to sit up in bed. Her head was

throbbing but she was worried. She didn't want the doctor to say that her dad was too ill to look after her, but seeing him collapsed on the settee had scared her. She knew deep down that he needed to get some help. 'You need to go to the doctor's Dad,' she said quietly. 'I'll be OK.'

Paul sat down on the end of her bed. He looked at her and frowned. 'I don't like to leave you on your own, especially as you're ill,' he said.

'I promise I'll ring the doctor's if there's an emergency,' said Megan trying to sound confident. 'But all I'm going to do is go to sleep.'

Paul sighed. 'OK,' he said. 'I'll try not to be long.'

Megan waited a few minutes after she heard the front door close, just to make sure her dad didn't come back for anything. Now was a good opportunity to put the envelope back where she had found it. She felt dizzy with sickness as she stood on the chair in her dad's room, but she gripped the box tightly as she lifted it down. The sketch book was still in there, but she felt so ill that she decided to leave it where it was for now. Putting the envelope on top of the sketch book, she put the box back on top of the wardrobe and returned to her room where she flopped down on her bed, dripping with perspiration.

She didn't hear her dad return. In fact, she didn't hear much at all that day, because she slept for most of the time. She spent the day in a blur of fever and confusion, sleeping fitfully, dreaming about cats and loud crashes. However, later in the evening she began to feel a little better. Her dad brought her some toast and tea and sat on her bed whilst she ate it. He seemed awkward and uncomfortable as he tried to chat about the weather and other inconsequential things and so it was some time before he finally said what he really wanted to say. 'The doctor has given me some tablets to calm me down a bit,' he muttered. 'Just to tide me over until I can see a counsellor.'

'Good,' was all Megan could think to say.

Paul smiled. He seemed relieved that she didn't ask him any questions and he left the room at the first opportunity. Megan was also relieved. She felt too ill for any more difficult conversations with her dad and she was glad there was no more mention of her going into care.

9

The Intruder

That same night, Paul went to bed earlier than usual and judging by his snoring, he quickly fell asleep. Megan wondered if the new tablets had made him drowsy. Although she still felt exhausted, she couldn't seem to sleep and it was almost midnight when she went downstairs for a drink of water. She was just getting the glass from the kitchen cupboard when she heard a noise coming from the back garden. It was a sharp bang, followed by a sort of rattling, creaking noise. When she parted the kitchen curtains, she saw a faint torchlight coming from Bill's shed. There was only a low fence between the two gardens, so she could see the shed quite clearly. She couldn't think what Bill would be doing in his shed at that time of night and she wondered why he hadn't put the light on. Then it occurred to her that it may not be Bill at all, but someone else.

'Dad wake up,' she called as she ran up the stairs. 'There's someone in Bill's shed.'

Paul was in a deep sleep and took some time to come round, but when he finally did, he quickly put on his shoes and raced downstairs towards the back door.

'Stay inside Megan,' he called as he ran outside, slamming the door shut behind him.

When Megan saw her dad sprinting over the low fence between the two houses, she wondered if she should call the police. She rushed into the hallway for the phone and was just thinking about picking up the handset, when she heard shouting from the garden. She ran back into the kitchen and looked across into Bill's garden. To her horror, she saw her dad grappling with a man outside the shed. Then she heard Bill's voice from out of the darkness. 'Get off my land or I'll shoot your legs off.'

The glint of a rifle butt caught her eye, as Bill waved a large gun in the direction of the shed. Then she heard Skippy barking and Ryan's voice, high pitched and panicking.

'No Grandad. Don't!'

Bill was distracted for a split second. 'Get back Ryan!' he shouted.

But a split second was long enough for the man to make his escape. He pushed Paul violently towards Bill, sending them both staggering backwards, but as Ryan ran to help them, the barrel of the gun caught the side of his face and he fell to the floor. Megan heard Ryan's cry of pain as the intruder jumped over the low fence and disappeared into the darkness.

Paul and Bill helped Ryan to his feet. His face was bleeding heavily and they took him inside. Megan could watch no more. She ran outside, jumped over the fence and ran into Bill's house. When she got there, her dad was phoning the police and Bill was holding a towel against Ryan's face. They all looked pale and shaken.

'I think it's just a split lip, Ryan,' said Bill shakily. 'Keep pressing on it 'til the bleeding stops.'

'The police are on their way,' said Paul when he eventually put the phone down.

Just then there was knock at the back door. A couple of neighbours had heard the commotion and had come to see if they could help. Bill said he was too upset to talk to anyone, so Paul went into the garden to reassure them that everything was under control and they left.

When he came back into the kitchen, he was carrying a mobile phone and the rifle that Bill had dropped in the scuffle. He placed them both carefully on the kitchen table.

'I think the police will be very interested in this phone I've just found,' he said, 'but we need to talk about the gun Bill.'

'What's to talk about?' said Bill abruptly. 'It's my old air rifle.'

Paul sighed. 'Yes, but you can't go round threatening people with it. It's a fire arm.'

Bill was becoming agitated. 'It's not a fire arm any more,' he said. 'The trigger's broken. I don't even have the pellets.'

'I hope the police understand that,' said Paul, 'because if they say it's a replica fire arm you're going to have some explaining to do.'

'Where did it come from?' asked Ryan from behind the towel.

'I keep it under my bed,' said Bill.

'Paul's right Grandad,' said Ryan, 'you shouldn't be threatening people with it.'

Bill looked angry and began to breathe heavily. 'He was an intruder on my land. It's my right to defend myself,' he said.

'OK Bill. Calm down,' said Paul. 'It's over now anyway. We're lucky none of us was badly hurt'.

Bill picked up his rifle. 'It belonged to my dad,' he said. 'I used to shoot tin cans with it when I was a lad and I'm not getting rid of it now, no matter what anyone says.'

No one spoke as Bill took his rifle upstairs and put it back under his bed.

'Did you get a close look at him Bill?' asked Paul, when Bill came back down.

'Yes, I did,' said Bill frowning. 'Did you?'

Paul nodded gravely. 'He was staggering when he came out of the shed. He must have been drinking.'

He glanced at Megan who was giving Ryan a drink of water and moved closer to Bill.

'I never thought he would stoop this low Bill, did you?' he whispered.

Bill lowered his voice. 'No, I didn't. I bet he was after the car parts. He should be locked up before he does any more damage.'

Paul moved nearer to Megan. 'I think you and Ryan should sit in the lounge for a bit,' he said, suddenly speaking normally again. 'Bill and I need to talk to the police in private when they come.'

'But they'll want to talk to me as well,' complained Ryan, now holding an ice pack to his face.

Paul helped Ryan up from the chair with a determined grip. 'They'll talk to you later,' he said firmly. 'Go on.'

Paul followed them to Bill's lounge and shut the door as he left, leaving them alone.

Megan was suspicious. It was obvious her dad and Bill didn't want to tell them who the intruder was. But it didn't matter because she thought she knew who it was anyway. She sat down next to Ryan on the settee and took deep breath before she spoke.

'I think it was Joe.'

Ryan put down the ice pack he was still holding to his face and stared at Megan.

'What?'

'I think the man in the shed was Joe,' she said again.

'What makes you say that?' said Ryan.

'He had black curly hair like Joe,' said Megan.

Ryan laughed. 'That's ridiculous Megan. Lots of people have black curly hair, and anyway it was dark and you never got that close to him.'

Megan couldn't explain how she knew it was Joe. She just did. But Ryan was right. It did sound ridiculous. She decided it was best not to say anything to the police about her own suspicions, but deep down she knew she was right.

Ryan's parents arrived just after the police had gone. Helena was her usual fussy self, but Ryan's dad Andy was calm and reassuring. Paul and Andy had been at school together and they greeted each other warmly. Bill was a little ashamed that he hadn't bought a new lock for the shed, but he was relieved to find there was no damage, apart from a broken lock, and nothing appeared to have been taken. After a while, both Andy and Bill thanked Paul for everything he had done and they parted on good terms. Megan was hopeful that this might heal the rift between Bill and her dad.

When they got home, the strain of the evening's events had taken their toll on both Megan and her dad. They were both so shocked and exhausted that they said very little to each other, before finally going to bed.

The ordeal in the garden had taken Megan's mind off how ill she was, but now she felt weak and sick. She decided she needed to get herself well again, so she could persuade her dad she was fit enough to go out with Ryan. This was the only way she could think of to get to Irene's house without her dad finding out. She climbed into bed and snuggled into the soft curves of the pillow. As she drifted off to sleep, another forgotten memory appeared. It was the soft feeling of warmth when her mother last kissed her face. It should have made her cry but it didn't. It just made her more determined than ever to seek out the truth.

Next day, neither Megan nor Ryan went to school. She was still too ill and Ryan was shaken up after the previous night's events. Paul was pleased when Megan started eating again, even if it was only small amounts, but she had yet to summon up enough courage to ask him if she could visit Ryan again.

A few days later, Megan and her dad were watching TV together in the lounge, when there was a knock at the door. It was Andy with a bottle of wine for Paul. Megan couldn't remember the last time anyone, other than Bill, had called to see her dad. He seemed to have cut himself off from any friends he once had. She was pleased to see her dad making Andy a cup of coffee and smiling. Paul and Andy spent some time talking about the old days when they were at school together, but eventually the conversation moved on to the house that Andy was building. It seemed he was having a problem with the electrician he had employed and so he asked if Paul would help him out some time. Megan knew this would be a big challenge for her dad. He hadn't worked as an electrician for such a long time that she thought he would refuse straight away, but to her surprise he said he would think about it and promised to let Andy know very soon.

'Ryan wanted to come with me today,' said Andy as he left, 'but he wasn't sure Megan was well enough for visitors.'

Megan looked pleadingly at her dad. 'She's getting better,' said Paul, smiling. 'Maybe Ryan can call round in a couple of days.' Megan felt a sense of great relief. Hopefully the ban on seeing Ryan was finally over.

During the next few days, Megan tried to eat a little more and sleep as much as she could and, as a result, her recovery was swift. Ryan had been allowed to visit her briefly one Saturday morning, even though her dad stayed in the room the whole time. But at least they had made contact again.

Soon after Ryan left, a red Mini pulled up outside Megan's house and Kirsty got out of the driving seat. She had heard that Megan was ill and had come to see how she was. Paul seemed a little nervous and overwhelmed by this visit, but he invited Kirsty into the house all the same. He spent some time talking about her car, telling her that he always had Minis himself in the past. Fortunately, Kirsty turned out to be a good listener as well as a good talker.

Megan noticed that her dad was becoming more relaxed as the conversation went on, which is something she hadn't seen in a long time. He even joked about how Megan had probably become ill because she wouldn't wear the padded coat he had bought for her. Megan pulled a face at the thought of it. Kirsty smiled knowingly.

'Dad's aren't always the best at choosing coats for teenage girls,' she said.

'She's not a teenager yet,' said Paul defensively.

'Well I nearly am,' said Megan.

'Maybe Megan can choose something for herself online,' suggested Kirsty.

Paul frowned. 'Megan's only allowed to use my laptop for school work,' he said, 'and I wouldn't know which sites we should look at for girls' clothes.'

'We usually just go to one of the high street stores,' said Megan, 'but Dad's not keen on shopping, so we don't spend much time choosing things.'

Kirsty was thoughtful for a moment. 'I'll let you know when I'm going shopping in York,' she said. 'Megan is welcome to come with me. I'm sure we can get a coat that's both warm and very cool if you see what I mean.'

As Kirsty laughed, Megan suddenly had a vague memory of her mother, laughing in this very same room and she realised that she hadn't heard the sound of laughter in this house for a very long time.

Momentarily distracted by this thought, Megan waited for Paul to refuse to let her go shopping with Kirsty. Whenever she was invited to go anywhere without her dad, he would refuse to let her go. But this time, to her astonishment, the refusal never came.

'Thanks Kirsty,' he said. 'Would you like that Megan?'

'That would be good,' replied Megan coolly. She tried not to sound too enthusiastic in case he changed his mind.

Kirsty looked pleased and winked at Megan. She could scarcely believe that a visit to York with Kirsty might actually happen.

Paul was keen to look at Kirsty's new car as she left. 'When was the last time you had a Mini?' asked Kirsty.

A heaviness hit Megan like a brick. She feared that this innocent question would drag Paul back into his world of anxiety. She thought he wouldn't answer, but she was wrong. 'I haven't owned one since my wife died several years ago,' he said, as he walked round the car. 'I gave up my job to look after Megan, so money was tight.'

'I'm sorry,' said Kirsty. 'I didn't mean to pry.'

'It's OK,' he replied gravely.

Kirsty got in the car and put down the window. 'I don't know anything about what's under the bonnet,' she said as she started the engine. 'Does it sound OK?'

'It purrs like a kitten,' said Paul.

'See you soon,' they all shouted as Kirsty drove away, and Megan really hoped that they would.

Paul seemed to have enjoyed Kirsty's visit as much as Megan had. In fact, after Kirsty left, Paul spent the rest of the day reading and listening to music, instead of going to bed like he often did in the afternoon.

10

Rosa

The night before Megan went to York with Kirsty, she spent hours trying on clothes. She just couldn't decide what to wear. Whatever she put on made her feel like a little girl and by the end of the evening she had grown to despise not only her clothes, but also her hair. She hated how her long red hair made her stand out from all the others at school. She wanted to have it cut short, but her dad wouldn't let her. She promised herself that she would dye it as soon as she was old enough to decide for herself.

The next morning, she pulled her hair tightly into a pony tail so her red hair would be less noticeable. She then put on a pair of jeans and the plainest sweatshirt she could find and went downstairs.

She got her waterproof jacket from the hallway and draped it over a chair in the kitchen, along with her bag. She wanted her dad to see that she would not be wearing her childish white padded coat, but for some reason he didn't seem to notice.

When Kirsty arrived in her Mini, she had braided her black hair with colourful strands, which Megan thought made her look like an African princess. Just before they left, Paul gave Megan some money to buy some new clothes. 'Make sure she gets a warm coat Kirsty,' he called as they set off, 'and look after her. She's all I've got you know.' Megan cringed. Her dad always said that and it was so embarrassing.

Kirsty chatted cheerfully as she drove the short journey to York. She talked about what sort of clothes would suit Megan's small frame and what colours would work with her red hair. Megan felt a warmth that she hadn't felt in a long time and she didn't want it to end.

The shops were dazzling to Megan. She loved the enticing window displays, the racks of colourful clothes and the pop music playing in the background. But what pleased her more than anything was the fact that she was there with Kirsty. It meant that, for once, she didn't stand out as the only girl in the shop with her dad. Although it was exciting, Megan also found it a little overwhelming, but Kirsty knew exactly what a twelve-year-old girl might like to wear. She didn't have a lot of money to spend, but by the end of the morning Megan had chosen a coat, a pair of jeans and two tops.

'We'd better go for some lunch now,' said Kirsty, 'and I know just where to go.'

Down one of the narrow lanes between the quaint York shops, there was a little Italian café. It had a shiny black floor and glass-topped tables that sparkled in the lights. Megan couldn't remember the last time she went out for something to eat. She wondered if she would understand the Italian menu, but she needn't have worried.

'Shall we both have pizza?' said Kirsty.

Megan felt proud to be with Kirsty. She had now dismissed Ryan's suspicions about her. In Megan's eyes, Kirsty could do no wrong. Not only was she a nice person, but she was also attractive to look at. Her tall slim figure, smooth black skin and braided black hair made her look stunning.

'Your hair looks lovely,' said Megan as they sat waiting for their food. 'I wish I knew what to do with mine,' she continued. 'I hate it being so red and curly.'

'Your hair is beautiful Megan,' said Kirsty emphatically. 'It's part of who you are,' she added. 'I used to try and iron my curls out with straighteners when I was younger, to make my hair look the same as everyone else's, but now I realise that's not what my hair is meant to look like.'

'I wish I could be strong like you,' sighed Megan.

'We're all different,' replied Kirsty. 'You're white skinned with red hair; I'm black skinned with black hair, but so what. It's what you're like inside that counts and you are a lovely girl Megan, both inside and out.'

Nobody had ever told Megan she was lovely before and even though she felt a bit embarrassed and didn't feel in the least bit lovely, she thought it was nice of Kirsty to say it.

A waitress with bright blue and purple streaks in her short black hair brought a coffee and a soft drink and placed them on the table. 'I'm afraid there's a 15-minute wait for the food,' she said politely. 'But just let me know if you want a free refill of your drinks and I'll get that for you.'

'She obviously doesn't mind looking different does she,' said Kirsty as she left, 'but she seems like a really nice person.'

Megan laughed. 'You're right,' she said.

Kirsty took off her coat and reached across the table for the coffee. Megan glanced at the terrible scars on her hand and arm and wondered again how they came to be there. She tried to look at them without Kirsty noticing but she failed.

'Are you wondering how I got these scars?' said Kirsty calmly.

Megan was embarrassed 'Sorry. I didn't mean…' she began.

Kirsty sipped her coffee. 'It's OK. It's only natural that people should wonder.'

She put down her cup and rolled back her sleeves, so Megan could see the full extent of the scars that spread upwards onto her arms. 'I got burnt,' she said quietly.

'How did it happen?' asked Megan.

112

'When I was a teenager we lived next door to a dog rescue centre. I used to take the dogs for walks and help out at weekends,' she explained. 'Then one evening the place caught fire. The poor dogs were trapped. They were barking and howling. Everyone was telling me to get back, but I just ran in to get them out and that's how I got the burns.' She paused and looked out of the window as her face saddened.

'Did you get the dogs out?' asked Megan.

'When the fire brigade arrived, they managed to free most of them,' said Kirsty 'but not all.' Her eyes welled up with tears. 'I lost my favourite dog,' she added. 'A greyhound called Peppy.'

Megan's mind flashed back to the fire in the woods and she began to understand why Kirsty had looked so shaken and behaved so strangely.

'I'm so sorry Kirsty,' said Megan. 'That must have been awful.'

'Yes, it was awful,' said Kirsty gravely. 'But the nurses in the hospital burns unit were great. That's why I raise money for them by running marathons.'

'How do you stay so cheerful having been through all that?' asked Megan.

'Well everyone copes with things differently,' answered Kirsty. 'But losing a dog isn't like losing your mother is it Megan? That must have been life-changing.'

It was the invitation to talk about her mother that Megan had been longing for. At last someone was not too scared to ask her how she felt. But now that moment had arrived she didn't know what to say.

'I don't remember much,' she muttered, 'I was only seven when she died.'

Fortunately for Megan, Kirsty was persistent. 'It was a car crash, wasn't it?' she asked gently.

'Yes. She was driving a car that hit a tree somewhere off the

York Road,' said Megan. 'My dad thinks she was distracted by something, but we don't know what.'

Kirsty sighed a deep sigh and shook her head as if in disbelief. 'Tragic,' she murmured. 'It's so tragic.'

Reaching out her scarred hand, Kirsty gently touched Megan's arm. 'It must have been hard for you and hard for your dad to cope with a seven-year-old as well as his own grief.'

Megan took a deep breath. She had to tell someone. She couldn't keep it to herself any longer. 'He's not well,' she said suddenly. 'There's something not right with him and I don't know what to do.'

Kirsty looked surprised. 'What do you mean?'

It was at that point that Megan began to tell someone what it was really like living with her dad. She told Kirsty about his tiredness, that left Megan doing all the housework. She told Kirsty about the times he would fly into a rage over nothing and the next minute he would be fine. Then she told her about his drinking until late into the night and how he sometimes never goes to bed. But most of all she told Kirsty how trapped she felt, as her dad tried to protect her from the world.

She spoke for quite a long time and for all that time Kirsty listened.

When Megan had finished, Kirsty spoke. 'Have you told anyone about this before?' she asked gently.

'No,' said Megan

Kirsty shifted around on her chair. She looked uncomfortable. 'Megan, has your dad ever … I mean has he ever…?' she began.

'My dad's never hurt me if that's what you mean,' said Megan. 'He would never do that.'

Kirsty looked relieved. 'That's good,' she murmured.

'You won't tell anyone will you Kirsty?' pleaded Megan. 'I don't want social services to take me away. That's what they do if your parents are too ill to look after you and you have no other relatives. I mean he's not really ill like he's got some disease or anything, is he?'

'He is ill Megan,' said Kirsty. 'But it's his mind that's ill isn't it?'

Megan nodded. 'He's got some tablets to calm him down until he sees a counsellor,' she said.

'I'm glad,' replied Kirsty. 'Talking to someone will help, but it can take a long time and it's not a magic cure.'

'The doctor said Dad may have to wait several months to see a counsellor,' said Megan.

'That's a long time to wait,' said Kirsty, 'but in the meantime, I'll see what I can do to help you.'

No more was said about her dad, but somehow Megan believed that Kirsty would indeed find a way to help, even though she had no idea what kind of help that would be.

When the pizzas arrived, they were huge and tasted wonderful, but Megan noticed that Kirsty kept looking at her watch. 'Do you have to go back soon?' asked Megan.

'No,' smiled Kirsty, 'but my cousin Beth said she might be here about now. She's just moved back to York from New Zealand and I haven't seen her since she got back.'

Megan looked surprised. 'Most people move from here to New Zealand, not the other way round.'

'It didn't work out,' said Kirsty. 'Beth missed her family and her daughter Rosa couldn't settle at school, so when her husband lost his job over there, they decided to come back. Oh, there she is,' she said, waving frantically across the café.

'Beth! Beth!' she shouted. 'Over here!'

A woman about Kirsty's age with short curly black hair rushed forward. Flinging herself enthusiastically at Kirsty, she hugged her with loud squeals. Her face looked a bit like Kirsty's, but she was much bigger.

Following quietly behind Beth was a tall thin girl with black curly hair tied back in a ponytail like Megan's. She looked at the floor, as if she was embarrassed at such a noisy reunion. 'Rosa! I hardly recognised you,' said Kirsty as she hugged the reluctant girl. 'You look so grown up all of a sudden.'

Rosa smiled politely but Megan thought she looked uncomfortable.

'This is my friend Megan,' said Kirsty, pulling two more chairs to the table.

'Hello,' said Beth warmly as she sat down. 'This is my daughter Rosa.'

Rosa smiled. 'Hi,' she whispered shyly.

'Hi,' said Megan.

Beth was as chatty as Kirsty. She spent the next few minutes describing all the details of their delayed flight from New Zealand, before deciding she'd better order some food.

'What do you want to eat Rosa?' asked Beth.

'You know what I want,' said Rosa abruptly.

'What's wrong with you Rosa?' asked Kirsty. 'You don't look very happy today.'

'She's mad at me because I won't buy her a phone,' said Beth in a loud voice. 'I'll just go to the ladies before I order. Do you need to go as well Rosa?'

Rosa looked embarrassed. 'No Mum. I can go on my own you know!'

'OK Miss independent,' said Beth as she left the table.

'I'll come with you,' said Kirsty. 'Get another menu for Rosa will you Megan.'

Megan took a menu from a nearby shelf and passed it to Rosa. 'Thanks,' said Rosa smiling, 'but I don't need it. I always have cheese and tomato pizza.'

'So do I,' said Megan.

Rosa put the menu down and turned to face Megan. 'Can I

ask you something?'

'Sure,' said Megan.

'Have you got your own phone?' she asked.

'No. My dad won't let me have one,' said Megan.

Rosa looked surprised. 'Really?' she said. 'In New Zealand, I was the only girl in my class who didn't have a phone.'

'Everyone's got them here too,' said Megan. 'Except me.'

'Mum says I have to wait 'til I'm thirteen,' said Rosa, 'but loads of girls get them when they're ten or eleven and I'm twelve.'

Megan was surprised that Rosa was only twelve, because she was so tall.

'I'm twelve as well,' said Megan. 'The girls in my class send messages and photos to each other on their phones all the time.'

'Do they lie about their age to get on the chat sites?' asked Rosa knowingly.

'Yeah. They just say they're thirteen or even older,' said Megan.

Rosa looked across the café as her mother and Kirsty burst out of the door marked Toilets, laughing hysterically. 'They're very embarrassing when they get together aren't they?' she said.

Megan grimaced. 'Look how everyone's staring at them.'

Rosa smiled. 'I should have brought my headphones.'

The girls watched as Kirsty and Beth went up to the cabinet where the desserts were displayed and stood for several minutes, drooling over the contents.

'What school do you go to?' asked Megan after a while.

'I haven't started yet,' said Rosa, 'but I'm going to York Academy next week.'

'I go there,' gasped Megan. 'Will you be in Year Eight?'

'Yeah. Is that your Year?' said Rosa excitedly.

Megan nodded. 'You might be in my form,' she said smiling, 'but if not I'll look out for you at break.'

'I'm glad I met you,' said Rosa. 'It's a bit scary starting a new school mid-year, when everyone's already made friends.'

'I haven't made any special friends yet,' said Megan, 'so I'll be your first friend.'

Rosa grinned broadly 'We'll be the only ones without a phone,' she said, 'but at least there are two of us.'

They spent another hour in the café, as Beth and Kirsty had a lot to talk about. But Rosa and Megan didn't mind. They sat together and chatted about school and music and clothes and it made Megan feel like a normal girl again. She couldn't remember exactly when she had become her father's carer, but that's what she felt like now.

When it was time to leave, Kirsty and Beth said a loud farewell outside the café and Megan arranged to meet up with Rosa at school.

There was a new spring in Megan's step as she walked back to the car with Kirsty.

'You seemed to get on well with Rosa,' said Kirsty.

'Yeah,' said Megan. ''We're going to meet up at school.'

Kirsty smiled. She climbed into the car and put on the radio. 'I love music,' she said.

Megan suddenly realised that she felt happy. She wished the day with Kirsty, Beth and Rosa would last forever, but the nearer they got to Oakton, the more Megan's happiness began to fade away and by the time they arrived at Megan's house, her happiness had almost disappeared.

Megan was relieved that Paul seemed in a good mood when he opened the door and to Megan's surprise, he invited Kirsty in for a cup of coffee. Megan was nervous. She began to worry that Kirsty would tell her dad what she had said about him. But Kirsty seemed very relaxed as Paul started to tell her about all the shops he worked in when he was an electrician in York.

'Why don't you try on your new clothes to show your dad,' suggested Kirsty as they drank their coffee.

When Megan took her bags upstairs, she could hear Kirsty and her dad laughing and chatting and she prayed that Kirsty would somehow be able to help.

'What do you think Paul?' asked Kirsty, when Megan appeared a few minutes later in some of her new clothes.

Paul gasped. 'You look just like your…' he hesitated before continuing, 'I mean you look so grown up,' he said sadly.

Kirsty laughed. 'No Paul. She doesn't look grown up. She looks just like a lovely girl of twelve should look.'

'You mean I've been dressing her like a little girl,' replied Paul smiling.

'You said it,' said Kirsty.

'You look really nice Megan,' said her dad. And that made Megan feel better than she had felt in a long time.

Megan couldn't wait to get to school the following week. She was hoping that Rosa would be in her form, but when she didn't appear at registration, Megan was bitterly disappointed. When it was time for the mid-morning break, Megan dashed to the back of the school gym, where she had arranged to meet Rosa. It was very busy round the back of the gym, but to Megan's great relief, Rosa appeared soon after she arrived. She was with a group of girls from one of the other Year Eight classes. Rosa left them as soon as she saw Megan and they greeted each other like long lost friends.

'I've been asked if I'd like a buddy to help me settle in,' said Rosa, as they walked together round the grounds.

'They always do that with new people,' said Megan. 'Who have you got?'

Rosa smiled. 'I asked if you could do it, because you are already my friend,' she said. 'Is that OK?'

Megan was delighted. 'Course it is,' she said.

At lunchtime, they met up again in the school café where Megan gave Rosa some advice on the best things to eat. They managed to find an empty table, but it wasn't long before Fern and Abbey from Megan's form came to sit with them. They had never wanted to sit with Megan before and Megan had taken a dislike to them, because they had once teased her about the colour of her hair.

Fern stared at Rosa. 'You're new, aren't you?' she said abruptly.

Rosa nodded.

'What year are you in?' asked Abbey, opening her sandwich.

'Year Eight,' said Rosa.

'You look too tall for Year Eight,' said Fern coldly.

'You look like a freaky giant sitting next to little Megan!' laughed Abbey.

Rosa looked upset. She said nothing but Megan was angry.

'So what if Rosa is tall. We're all different,' said Megan. 'It's what someone's like as a person that really matters,' she added.

'Only trying to be friendly,' said Abbey. 'Come on Fern, if these freaks don't want to be our friends we'll sit somewhere else.'

'Thanks for sticking up for me,' said Rosa after they'd gone, 'but I hope you're not going to lose your friends because of me.'

'They're not my friends,' said Megan. 'They never have been and I'm glad they won't bother us again.'

Rosa looked up as a small boy sat down at the end of the table holding a bag of crisps.

'You're the new girl in my form, aren't you?' he said to Rosa.

Megan sighed. It was going to be a long lunchtime.

'I'm Ben,' he said, 'but they call me The Face because I'm good at pulling faces.'

Rosa laughed. 'This is my friend Megan.'

'Hi Megan,' he said warmly. 'Do either of you want this bag of crisps? I've just bought the wrong flavour and they're yukky.' He pulled such a funny face that both Rosa and Megan burst out laughing as they declined his offer. 'See you later then,' he said, as he got up and left.

'I think you've got a boyfriend Rosa,' said Megan.

'No, I think you have!' said Rosa. 'He's far too short for me.'

Megan laughed. It was so good to have a friend to share things with, but there were things she couldn't really tell Rosa about at the moment and maybe she never would. When she was with Rosa she felt like she was in another world. She felt like an ordinary twelve-year-old girl and she didn't want anything to spoil that feeling.

Ryan was the only person who knew about her problems and she began to wonder when she would be seeing him again.

'What are you thinking about?' asked Rosa. 'Have those girls upset you?'

'No. I'm OK,' said Megan quickly. 'Let's go and find where your next lesson is.'

11

Tom

Several days later Megan got back from school to find her dad just finishing a conversation on the phone. 'That was Andy,' he told her. 'He's asked me if I'll help him with the electrics at his new house this weekend and I've said I will.'

Megan was delighted. 'That's great Dad.'

'If it's OK with Bill, you can stay at his house for the day, whilst I'm at Andy's,' said Paul. 'I don't want to leave you in the house all day on your own.'

'That's fine with me,' said Megan, trying not to sound too keen. She knew this would be a good opportunity to visit Irene with Ryan and she couldn't believe her luck.

When the day came for Paul to go to Andy's house he seemed very nervous. Megan knew what a big thing it was for him to go to work after being so long at home, but he soon calmed down when Andy arrived to pick him up.

Paul watched from Andy's car as Megan made her way to Bill's house. He wanted to make sure she was OK before he left.

When Ryan opened the door, he looked on edge.

'Is something wrong?' asked Megan as they went into the lounge.

'No but I've got something to tell you,' he said.

Bill followed them into the room. 'Just make yourself at home Megan,' he said warmly.

'I'll go and put the kettle on.'

Ryan waited for Bill to leave the room before he spoke. 'You were right Megan,' he said. 'The police are looking for Joe Hawkins. They want him for questioning.'

Megan looked surprised. 'How do you know?'

'Ray came round to see Bill last night,' said Ryan. 'He was really upset. He said the police had been to his garage asking if he knew where Joe was, but no-one's seen him. He's gone to ground. Just disappeared.'

Megan wondered if her dad and Bill had told the police that it was Joe in the shed.

'I bet he's hiding in the woods somewhere,' said Ryan. 'He goes running there doesn't he?'

'Yes. He was there on the day of the fire.' said Megan.

Ryan looked surprised, like he'd had a lightbulb moment. 'It could have been Joe's cigarette that started the fire,' he exclaimed. 'There was an empty cigarette packet on the path by the watchtower. He could have been smoking, when he was taking the stolen goods away. He just stubs the cigarettes out on the ground. We saw him doing that at the Hall. If he didn't put his cigarette out properly, then whoosh, the woods would catch fire.'

Megan was now catching up with Ryan's thinking. 'Do you think that was Joe's cigarette packet in Sarah's Frog-Eyed Sprite? I bet they drive to work together now they both work at the Hall.'

Ryan was becoming more and more animated as they spoke. 'Yes, it must be his. Remember how Kirsty pushed the packet back into his pocket. It all makes perfect sense now.'

Megan was still thinking it all through, but Ryan was convinced he was right. 'Just think about it Megan. The watchtower's a perfect place to hide stolen stuff, until you're ready to sell it on. He stole the key so no-one else could get in there.'

'Apart from the cat,' said Megan lightly.

Their conversation stopped abruptly when Bill came in with some tea and a plate of cakes, followed closely by Skippy. 'I bought these chocolate cakes especially for you Megan,' he said, as he put them on a table. They used to be your favourites, when you were a little girl.'

'Thanks Uncle Bill. They still are,' said Megan, 'but we'd better make sure Skippy doesn't eat these like she did the biscuits.'

Skippy wagged her tail as Bill threw her a piece of cake. 'That's it Skippy. No more,' he said firmly, as she gobbled it up.

'We were just talking about Joe Hawkins,' said Ryan.

Bill looked uncomfortable. 'He's a hot head,' he muttered angrily.

Megan was curious. 'How do you know him Uncle Bill?' she asked.

'I was working at Rays Garage when Sarah married Joe,' said Bill.

'What do you mean, he's a hot head?' asked Ryan.

'He used to be in the army,' said Bill. 'I think he'd seen some action in the Far East that messed his mind up.'

Bill shook his head gravely before continuing. 'The same thing happened after both the First and Second World Wars. Men who'd seen fighting were like different people when they got home.'

'How were they different?' asked Megan.

'They were on a short fuse,' explained Bill. 'They'd lose their tempers the minute something went wrong and then spend days not talking. The memories of what they saw would never go away you see.'

'Didn't anyone try to help them?' asked Ryan.

'Oh, there was none of this fancy counselling stuff in those days,' said Bill, 'and I'm not sure it's much better for our soldiers now,' he added.

'Did Joe get any help?' asked Megan.

'I've no idea,' replied Bill. 'He'd left the army by the time he met Sarah. He was out of work when they got married, so Ray set him on at his garage as an apprentice. He worked there with me for a while, but I couldn't cope with him. He would fly into a rage if things didn't go right and he thought he could just do what he wanted. I felt sorry for him, but when he got into a fight with one of the customers Ray fired him.'

Bill looked upset and took a large gulp of his tea before abruptly changing the subject.

'Why don't you take Skippy for a walk,' he suggested. 'It's stopped raining at last.'

'Good idea,' said Ryan.

'Oh, by the way,' said Bill suddenly. 'Did you hear about the big cat that's been sighted in Oakton woods. It was on the news last night. They think it's a cougar or a puma or something like that. A woman saw it last week, when she was walking her dog and now a second person has seen it as well.'

Megan's face went pale.

'Did they say it was dangerous?' asked Ryan.

'Well it's obvious you wouldn't want to come face-to-face with a big cat, would you Ryan?' said Bill. 'They're killers. Of course it's dangerous. You just have to keep away from the woods until they catch it, that's all.'

'Who's trying to catch it?' asked Megan.

'I can't remember what they said on the news,' said Bill, 'but if it's not caught soon they'll be bringing in the army to hunt it down I expect.'

Megan was becoming more alarmed as the conversation went on, but she tried not to show it. 'What will they do if they catch it?' she asked.

'They'll probably try shooting it with one of those tranquillizer darts,' said Bill, 'but if that doesn't work and they think it may harm someone, they'll have to shoot it.'

'No,' said Ryan. 'They can't do that. It's not fair. It won't harm anyone unless it feels threatened.'

Bill looked surprised. 'I didn't know you were such a cat lover Ryan,' he said.

'I'm not,' said Ryan quickly. He didn't want Bill to become suspicious, but the thought of the army hunting down Tom and Zoe made him very angry.

Megan came to his rescue. 'Thanks for telling us Uncle Bill,' she said calmly. 'We'll be careful.'

'Good,' said Bill. 'Skippy is looking at her lead right now, so I think she's keen to go out whenever you are.'

Ryan and Megan didn't need asking again. They couldn't wait to leave.

Neither of them spoke until they were far enough away from Bill's house to talk freely.

'Do you think Irene's heard the news about the big cat sightings?' asked Megan.

'I hope so,' said Ryan, 'but if Zoe and Tom are roaming the woods at the moment, there's not a lot she can do to protect them.'

'What will she do if they come back?' said Megan.

Ryan shrugged his shoulders. 'Try to lock them in the pens I suppose.'

'But she can't keep them in the pens forever,' said Megan. 'They're wild. They need to be free.'

Ryan kicked a stone along the pavement as he walked. There was a feeling of foreboding in the air, as if something bad was about to happen and there was nothing they could do about it.

When they reached the turning onto the woodland path they both stopped and stared.

There was a notice on a tree, warning walkers about the sightings of a big cat, along with a number to phone if anyone should see it. 'Come on,' said Megan. 'We've got to make sure Irene knows about this. I hope she's at home.'

'And let's hope no-one else sees the cats in the meantime,' said Ryan. 'Come on Skippy. Let's run.'

Skippy was delighted and set off running with great enthusiasm, but by the time they reached the woodyard, the old dog was getting tired. Ryan stroked her head as they slowed down to a walk. 'Not far now Skippy. Come on old girl.' But as they approached the gatehouses Skippy's behaviour suddenly changed. She began to bark furiously and pull on her lead. Ryan hauled her back. 'Maybe there's a rabbit or something nearby,' he said.

'We'll have to keep her inside the house if Zoe's in the pen,' said Megan. 'We don't want either of them to get scared.'

Ryan laughed. 'I think Skippy is the only one who'll be scared.'

'What a surprise,' smiled Irene on opening the door. 'I've been wondering how you two were getting on.'

'Have you seen the news?' asked Ryan as soon as they walked in.

'You mean about the big cat sightings?' she said.

They both nodded.

'Yes, I have,' she replied gravely. 'I've shut Zoe in her pen for now, but I'm really worried about Tom. He hasn't been back for food for several days now and it's not like him.'

As they sat down in the small sitting room, Megan's eyes automatically checked the shelf for the photo. She was pleased to see that it was still there, along with all the other cat ornaments and the basket of knitted cats.

'Grandad says they could get the army in, if they get more sightings,' warned Ryan. 'Tom could be captured or shot. What are we going to do?'

'There's not much we can do at the moment,' said Irene.

'But I'm going to see if I can locate Tom today and then try to lure him back to the pen with some meat.'

'And then what?' said Ryan.

'Keep them in the pens until all the excitement dies down I suppose,' said Irene. 'But I've got to find Tom first.'

As they sat gloomily in the sitting room, Skippy lay down in front of the fire and began to fall asleep. 'Anyway, how's Zoe?' asked Megan.

'Come and have a look for yourself,' said Irene. She looked at the sleeping dog and smiled. 'We can leave Skippy to her dreams for a while,' she said.

Zoe was in one of the pens. Although she didn't look ill, Irene was obviously worried about her. Zoe's stomach was swollen and Irene said she had noticed some white fluid on the cat's bedding that morning. 'She wouldn't eat anything last night,' said Irene sadly.

'Why don't you call the vet?' asked Ryan, trying to be helpful.

Irene shook her head. 'With all this scaremongering about big cats on the loose, I don't want anyone to know I've got a sick wild cat. People can be cruel if they feel threatened or scared,' she added. 'Goodness knows what would happen if the newspapers got hold of a picture of these pens.'

Megan shuddered at the thought of the wild cats being hunted down, just because people were scared of them. She knew what it would do to Irene if they were harmed.

'Come on,' said Irene. 'We can't do any more. Let's go back inside.'

Skippy was still asleep when they returned, so Irene made them a drink. Megan had been distracted by the cat sightings, but she hadn't forgotten why she wanted to see Irene. She thought maybe this was a good time to get some answers to her questions.

'Irene,' she said tentatively as they sipped their drinks, 'I found an old newspaper cutting the other day.'

Ryan looked taken aback. Megan hadn't told him anything about a news cutting.

Irene's lined face twisted into a scowl, as if she sensed what Megan was going to say.

'It had a photo of the car my mum crashed in and it was here, just outside your house.' said Megan.

There was no big response from Irene, but she nodded slightly as she looked at the floor.

This small nod made Megan feel a little braver and she decided to carry on.

'Dad's Mini was outside your house, but the newspaper report said she was driving a sports car. I don't understand.'

Irene's eyes drifted upwards to the photo of Megan and her mother on the shelf. When she started to speak her voice came out in a whisper, but Megan listened hard. Now she had got this far, she wanted to make sure she heard every single word.

'You and your mum were on the way to York that day in the Mini,' said Irene still speaking softly, 'but you called at my house on the way, so I could give you your birthday present.'

There was a pause as Irene sighed heavily. Megan hardly dare move. She realised that Irene could easily change her mind and refuse to tell her any more. Megan was very relieved when she eventually carried on.

'When it was time for you to leave my house, the Mini wouldn't start,' said Irene.

'Your mum rang Ray at the garage, but he was out at a classic car rally with Bill. He'd left the new apprentice in charge, but he wasn't a qualified mechanic, so the Mini couldn't be fixed.'

'Why didn't you take them to York in your own car?' asked Ryan.

'Because Mike had gone to work in it,' she answered.

Irene shifted around in her chair, as if she wanted to be somewhere else. Any mention of her husband Mike seemed to upset Irene greatly and Megan felt there was a danger that she would stop talking because of that. Some-how she needed to encourage her to carry on.

'It's OK Irene,' she said reassuringly, 'I know most of what happened already, but I just need to know a few more details.'

Ryan raised his eyebrows in amazement at such exaggeration, but Irene didn't notice. Her face had just visibly relaxed. 'I'm glad your dad has seen sense at last,' she said.

Megan didn't see any harm in letting Irene think her dad had now told her most of the truth, even if he hadn't. She also decided to take things a little slower.

'I can't remember why Mum had to go to York on my birthday,' said Megan, trying to appear calm. 'Was she going to buy me a present or something?'

Irene's face was almost back to normal now, as she began to recall some of the happier moments before the crash. 'She was going to collect a special birthday cake for you,' she said. 'Your dad should've picked it up on his way back from work the night before, but he was so busy that he forgot. Your mum wasn't too pleased about that,' she laughed.

'I still have the birthday card she sent me,' said Megan trying to smile.

Irene got up and walked over to a cupboard. 'Do you know I think I still have the one I gave you somewhere,' she said, opening a drawer. 'You left it behind, so I kept it.'

Irene began to rummage through a drawer in the cupboard. 'I'm not sure where I put it now. Never mind. I'll keep looking.'

Skippy growled in her sleep. 'She's dreaming of chasing cats,' said Irene as she closed the drawer.

Ryan was getting frustrated at the slow pace of everything.

He was desperate to find out the truth. 'How come Maggie ended up driving a sports car?' he asked bluntly.

'Ray's apprentice lent it to her,' said Irene. 'It was one of those Frog-Eyed Sprites that Ray was so keen on.'

Megan was annoyed at Ryan. She knew he was only trying to help, but she felt that he was maybe pushing Irene too hard for answers.

'If she drove to York and back in the Sprite,' asked Ryan again, 'why didn't Megan go with her? There are two seats in the car.'

Irene answered quickly. 'Megan wanted to stay with me and play with her birthday present,' was her explanation. On the surface, this seemed a perfectly good reason for Maggie to leave Megan behind and travel alone, but there was something in Irene's manner that made Megan think this was not quite the whole truth. She was becoming more and more flustered. As her expression began to change, she looked directly at Megan. 'Does your dad know you're here?' she asked.

Megan felt a pang of guilt. Not only had she deceived Irene about how much she knew, but she had also deceived her dad. She just didn't know what to say.

Ryan, however was becoming angry. 'No,' he said defiantly, 'Megan's dad doesn't know we are here and neither does my grandad, but Megan needs your help Irene. All she wants to know is the truth. She's going to find out everything eventually, so why won't you tell her now?'

The sound of Ryan's raised voice roused Skippy from her sleep and he bent down to stroke her. There was something comforting about the old dog that soothed him in moments like these.

Megan was close to tears by now. Ryan was right. She would never stop trying to find out exactly what happened to her beloved mother, no matter how long it took.

Irene looked again at Megan's troubled face. 'None of this is your fault Megan,' she said kindly. 'Your dad just wants to protect you that's all, but I'm in a difficult position, because I don't know how much he's told you.'

Ryan was becoming more and more frustrated the more he heard. 'Megan knows she wasn't in the sports car when it crashed,' he cried, 'but she needs to know if she actually saw the crash. Why can't you just tell her that?'

'The truth is Megan, I don't know,' said Irene earnestly. 'We were playing hide and seek in the house. I didn't notice the back door was open and whilst I was counting, you went into the garden, opened the gate and went into the woods to hide.'

'I remember you calling my name,' said Megan, her voice trembling, as the hidden memories came flooding back. 'I was hiding when I saw a cat.'

'What cat?' asked Ryan.

'It was Tom wasn't it Megan?' said Irene. 'I saw him too. He was in the woods just before the crash.'

Megan put her hands to her head. Suddenly, she could remember the crashing sound that rang through the woods, but she had no memory of seeing it. Was this what her dad wanted to protect her from? Did he think she might have seen the crash? Did he want to stop her from uncovering a hidden memory that was best left forgotten?

Irene came across and put her arm round Megan. 'I don't think you saw it happen Megan. You came from round the back of the garden, when you heard the crash.'

'Is that why my dad is so angry with you?' asked Megan, 'because he thinks you let me go into the woods, where I might have seen the crash.'

Irene wiped away a tear.

Megan took a deep breath. 'If it wasn't me who distracted my mum, then could it have been the cat?'

Irene nodded.

'Did my mum know about Tom?' said Megan.

'Yes,' said Irene. 'She loved Tom, but like me, she feared for his safety if anyone found out he was a wild cat.'

'If Tom ran in front of the car, would she swerve to avoid him?' asked Megan.

'Yes,' said Irene, 'she would.'

It was now Megan's turn to wipe away a tear.

'If it was my cat who distracted Maggie,' said Irene softly, 'then it was my fault she died wasn't it?'

Megan suddenly felt sorry for Irene, but there was nothing more she could say.

Ryan had kept quiet during all this, but there was still something that didn't quite make sense.

'Was Joe Hawkins the apprentice?' he asked.

Irene looked surprised. 'Yes, he was,' she said hesitantly.

'Well, why would he lend Maggie the Sprite?' he continued. 'It was an expensive classic car from Ray's Garage. I can't believe he would lend her a car like that.'

Irene frowned. She seemed irritated. 'I've told you all I dare tell you,' she said. 'If you want to know any more, you will have to ask Paul.' She moved towards the door. 'You'll have to go now,' she said abruptly. 'I have to get some meat ready, if I'm going to look for Tom.'

'She's holding something back,' muttered Ryan, as Irene closed the door behind them and although she was grateful for everything Irene had told her, Megan had to agree.

12

The Fugitive

Black clouds were beginning to fill the sky, darkening the woods with slanting rain. As they walked away from Irene's house, Skippy began to growl fiercely and pull on the lead. 'I think she can sense a storm coming,' said Ryan. But when she began to pull even more, the lead suddenly slipped out of his hands. Within seconds, the dog darted across the path and disappeared round the back of the empty gatehouse, on the other side of the stone arch.

'Skippy!' they both shouted together, but there was no response. 'It's the greyhound blood in her,' said Ryan, as they ran after her. 'She's always chasing after something.'

Stepping around the building materials strewn across the front garden, they made their way to the back of the empty gatehouse. The glass in the back door had been smashed, leaving a nice convenient hole for Skippy to jump through.

'Skippy!' shouted Ryan through the hole. A noise coming from inside the house startled them. It was a slamming sound, like a door closing, followed by the sound of barking and whining. It sounded like Skippy was scratching frantically at something hard. Ryan lowered his head to step through the broken glass door.

'Wait,' said Megan, taking hold of the door handle. She gave a push and the door swung open. 'The lock's been broken. Someone's been here before.'

The blinds in the house were closed. Megan wished she had brought her torch. They stopped and listened. They could still hear Skippy scratching and whining. They listened again. The sound seemed to be coming from upstairs. With careful steps, they slowly climbed each creaky wooden stair, until they came to a landing, where Skippy was growling and scratching at one of the doors. Ryan made a grab for her lead. 'What is it Skippy? Is it a rat? He tried to pull Skippy away, but she just didn't want to move. He put his hand on the door handle. 'You won't be satisfied until I let you take a look, will you?'

The minute Ryan opened the door, Skippy dragged him in, followed closely by Megan.

Then a man's voice came out of the shadows. 'Get that dog away, before I kick it away!'

Ryan grabbed Skippy by the collar and pulled her back, as the man pushed past them and made for the open door. But then he stopped unexpectedly and turned to face them. In the faint backlight of the open door, Megan saw the outline of a man with thick curly hair.

Sit over there on the floor where I can see you,' ordered the man, pointing to the window. He took out a small torch and shone it at the cowering pair.

'Megan!' he said. 'What are you doing here?'

'Joe!' said Megan.

Joe stepped back into the room, closing the door firmly behind him.

'Don't be scared,' he said gently. 'I won't hurt the dog if you keep it under control.'

Ryan didn't believe him. He was afraid for Skippy's safety. He remembered his grandad's words about Joe's quick temper and tried to quieten Skippy by stroking her under her chin.

Joe put his torch on the floor, lighting up the room with an eerie glow. He looked tired and anxious. 'I'm so sorry to involve you in all this Megan,' he said, shaking his head.

Then he swung round angrily to face Ryan. 'If you'd kept that dog on a lead,' he cried, 'Megan wouldn't have got into this situation would she!'

Megan jumped to his defence. 'He did have her on a lead, but she just pulled away. It wasn't his fault.'

'OK, OK,' said Joe. 'Just let me think about what to do now.'

Ryan rose to his feet. 'Do you know the police are looking for you?' he said.

'Sit down,' said Joe gruffly. He picked up his torch and shone it fully in Ryan's face.

'You're Bill's grandson, aren't you?'.

Ryan sat back down on the floor. 'Yes,' he hissed, 'and it was my grandad's shed you were stealing from.'

Skippy growled as Joe took a step towards Ryan and towered over him.

'You'd better keep your mouth shut,' he said menacingly. 'I'm in no mood for loud-mouthed lads.' He pointed his finger at Ryan. 'Just keep hold of your dog and keep quiet. I need to talk to Megan about something.'

Megan was scared for Ryan's safety. Joe seemed touchy and easily angered. She thought if she tried to keep Joe talking, he might calm down a little.

'What do you want to talk to me about Joe?' she asked.

'I don't suppose your dad told you what was in my letters,' said Joe after a pause.

'No,' said Megan, 'I didn't even know they were from you, until you told me.'

'He always was a fool,' said Joe bitterly. 'What has he told you about me?'

'Nothing. That's the trouble,' she replied. 'But I think I might have met you before, when I was younger.'

She couldn't see Joe very well in the semi-darkness, but she could sense a kind of warmth when he talked to her.

'Your mum used to bring you to Ray's Garage, when I worked there,' he said. 'You used to like sitting in the Frog-Eyed Sprites.'

'You lent Maggie one of those didn't you?' said Ryan.

'I thought I told you to keep quiet,' said Joe viciously.

'Don't get mad at him,' pleaded Megan. 'He's been trying to help me find out about my mum. No-one will tell me the truth about what happened to her.'

Joe sighed. 'Your mum would want you to know what happened. I know she would.'

'Can you tell me what you know then?' asked Megan.

Joe looked at Megan. 'I didn't *lend* your mum the car,' he said. 'I drove her to York in it. It was my chance to drive one of the Sprites without Ray checking up on me. Why should I stay at the garage, when both Ray and Bill were having a day off at a car rally? I was supposed to be an apprentice, but they treated me like dirt.'

Ryan was annoyed at such criticism of his grandad. 'Why didn't you get another job then, if they were so bad?' he said.

Joe bowed his head. His voice was low and full of pain. 'Because no-one wants to employ a killer,' he said.

There was a silence before Megan spoke again. Her voice was trembling. 'What do you mean Joe? Have you killed someone? Who have you killed?'

Joe ran his hands nervously through his curly hair. He looked unsettled and uneasy. 'When you throw grenades and drop bombs, you know you've killed people,' he said, 'but you don't know who they are. They're just the enemy. If you don't kill them, they'll try to kill you … but that doesn't make it any easier.'

In the quiet of the room, Megan could hear Joe breathing

rapidly, as if he couldn't catch his breath. Tension hung in the air like choking dust.

'Maggie said the army would make a man of me,' said Joe, after a while, 'but in the end, it did just the opposite.'

Ryan looked angry. 'Lots of people have a hard time in the army, but they don't steal things,' he said.

Joe spun round and put his face near to Ryan's. 'You've got plenty to say for yourself haven't you,' he said threateningly. 'Just let me give you some advice. Don't accuse people of things, unless you've got evidence,' he yelled. 'Now just button it, while I finish talking.'

He moved away from Ryan and went back to sit in front of the door. 'What else do you want to know Megan?' he asked.

Megan was becoming more and more afraid for Ryan, but after all this time, she knew exactly what she wanted to know.

'If you drove my mum to York and back, then why was she driving alone when she crashed?' she asked.

'Your mum was a very persuasive woman,' said Joe. 'She was pestering me all the way back from York to let her drive the Sprite. So, when we turned off the York Road into Oakton woods, I said she could drive it from there. I didn't see any harm in it. It was a private road and there were no other cars about. But Maggie being Maggie, she insisted on driving it on her own, so I got out and left her to it.'

'Did you see what made her crash?' asked Megan nervously.

'I was walking behind the car,' said Joe. 'That particular Sprite had a more powerful engine than most of them and she was driving too fast.'

His voice began to break as he revealed what happened next. 'She was going too fast, but she would have been OK, if she hadn't suddenly swerved.'

'Did you see what made her swerve?' asked Megan.

'Not really,' he replied. 'But I saw Irene running out of her house after it happened and then I saw you running from behind the garden and Irene scooping you up and carrying you inside.'

There was a long silence.

'It's my fault she died,' said Joe tearfully. 'If I hadn't let her drive the Sprite, she would still be alive now. I'm so sorry.'

Megan didn't know what to say. She had found out the truth at last and yet she was not entirely satisfied. She was having disturbing thoughts about her mother's relationship with Joe. She couldn't understand why her mum had been seeing such a lot of him and she was beginning to think it may be better not to know.

Joe looked up, as if he had almost read her thoughts.

'Megan,' he said. 'Do you know who I am?'

Megan didn't know why she hadn't made the connection before. She had become so focused on the events surrounding the crash that she had missed some very important information. Joe's last name was Hawkins. It was the name she had seen on her mum's birth certificate.

'Maggie was my sister,' said Joe swallowing hard. 'She was my big sister. Apart from Sarah, she was the only person who cared about what happened to me after I came out of the army.'

Megan was speechless. Joe was her uncle and her dad had not wanted her to know.

'When your mum died, your dad didn't want you to have anything to do with an uncle like me,' said Joe sadly. 'And I can't say I blame him. But I've got a daughter of my own now and she needs to know who her cousin is. None of this is her fault, or yours, so why should you both suffer?'

'Is that what the letters were about?' asked Megan.

'Yes,' said Joe. When I saw you with Kirsty that day, I recognised you straight away. You look just like Maggie and I yearned for you to meet my daughter Alice. It's not her fault she's got such a mixed-up dad. I wrote to your dad, asking him if you could meet your cousin, but he never replied.'

There was so much more Megan wanted to ask, but the situation was bad. Joe was a wanted man and she knew that Ryan would call the police as soon as they got out of the house.

'How long are you going to keep us here?' said Ryan.

Joe stood up and moved away from the door. 'I'm not keeping you here,' he said. 'I'm not into kidnapping children, least of all my own niece. You can go when you want.'

Ryan got up, still holding Skippy's collar. The dog had calmed down by now and was even wagging her tail at Joe. Megan got up to join them, but as they moved towards the door, Joe put his arm across it, barring the way.

'I need you to help me first,' he said.

Ryan still felt afraid. He didn't trust Joe one bit.

'I know you'll call the police as soon as you leave here,' said Joe, 'but I need some time to explain things to Sarah first and I need a phone to call her on. I must have dropped mine when I ran off.'

Ryan didn't believe him, but he said nothing.

'I'm sorry Megan, but I need you both to empty your pockets and hand me your phones,' said Joe.

'My dad won't let me have a phone,' said Megan, as she emptied her pockets. Joe took Ryan's phone from him and put it in his pocket. 'I need to make sure you won't call the police as soon as you leave here,' he said. 'They'll find out the truth soon enough. I just need time to call Sarah before I talk to them, that's all,' he added. 'She doesn't deserve all this. The least I can do is try to explain.'

He looked at Ryan. 'Don't worry, you'll get your phone back. I'll leave it here for the police to find.'

Ryan still wasn't convinced that Joe was telling the truth about anything, but he wasn't going to argue with him. 'Can we go now?' he asked.

'You can do what you like,' said Joe.

Megan was still in shock. It had been a lot to take in. She followed Ryan through the door in silence, until Joe called after her. 'My little lass looks a lot like you. We've all got the same red curly hair, only I dye mine black.'

Megan stopped. 'What did you say her name was?'

'Alice,' said Joe. 'Alice Maggie Hawkins. She was born just after your mum died, so we gave her Maggie as her middle name.'

Joe watched them as they descended the stairs and walked away from the house. Ryan had planned to phone the police from Irene's house, but her car wasn't there, so he kept on walking. Megan looked back at the empty gatehouse. She should have been pleased that at last she had discovered the whole truth about what happened on her seventh birthday, but she felt empty. She had just found an uncle and a cousin, but things being the way they were, she may not see Joe again or meet little Alice. She thought that if Joe was found guilty of all those burglaries he was likely to end up in prison and her dad would never agree to let her visit him there. But something Joe had said to Ryan about evidence, made her wonder if Joe was innocent after all. She consoled herself with the thought that, somewhere nearby, she had a little cousin called Alice Maggie, who would be about five years old by now. Just a bit younger than she was when all these bad things started to happen that changed her life.

When they got to the woodyard, Ryan began to run. 'Come on Megan,' he cried. 'We've got to get home and call the police.'

Megan hung back. 'Joe needs time to call Sarah,' she answered.

'Don't be so naive Megan,' said Ryan. 'That was just a trick to give him time to get away.'

Megan was confused. She knew Joe had probably committed all these crimes and yet she wondered if it was all a mistake. His life was in a mess, but all she could think of was the effect it was going to have on little Alice.

When they arrived at Bill's house he called the police immediately. Bill seemed to blame Joe for everything. He told Megan how Paul wanted Maggie to stay away from her brother Joe, after he came out of the army. 'We all felt sorry for him at first,' said Bill. 'He'd seen a lot of bad things in the army, but he was so angry with everyone that people were scared of him.'

'Was my mum scared of him?' asked Megan.

'No,' laughed Bill. 'Maggie wasn't scared of anyone. She still saw quite a lot of Joe, despite what Paul said.'

'But why didn't my dad keep in contact with Joe, after my mum died?' asked Megan. 'He's still my uncle, no matter what he's like.'

Bill tried his best to explain. It was too late now to hide anything.

'When your dad found out that Joe had let your mum drive that Sprite, he partly blamed him for the crash,' said Bill. 'He told Joe he never wanted to see him again.'

'Maybe we should let Irene know about Joe,' interrupted Ryan. 'He could be dangerous and he might still be in the gatehouse.'

'I doubt it,' sneered Bill. 'He's probably half way to York by now, with your phone.'

'The police can trace mobile phones,' said Megan. 'I don't think he'll use Ryan's if he goes on the run.'

It wasn't long before Paul and Andy returned. As their car drew up outside, Megan felt a sense of panic. 'Will you tell my dad what's happened, Uncle Bill,' she pleaded. 'I can't face him.'

'OK,' said Bill. 'I'll talk to them in the kitchen.'

Bill was gone for some time, leaving Megan and Ryan to talk over everything that had happened to them over the past few months.

When Paul finally came into the room, he put his arm round Megan. 'I've made a bit of a mess of things haven't I Megan?' he said gently. 'But things are going to change from now on. I promise.'

'He's got himself a job on my building site,' said Andy. 'I vote him the best electrician round here.' Megan smiled politely. She hoped things would get better for her dad, but she knew he didn't always keep his promises.

That night Megan spoke to her dad about Irene and told him how she would like them to make peace with each other. 'Irene has apologised for taking her eyes off me that day,' said Megan. 'I know I heard the crash, but I didn't see anything.'

Paul listened carefully before replying. 'I can't promise everything will be OK, just like that,' he said slowly. 'Feelings run too deep to change overnight, but I do promise to write to Irene. I'll ask her if she would like to talk.'

Megan was pleased, but she didn't mention anything about Joe. She was too exhausted to tackle anything more and that night they both had a warm drink and went to bed early.

13

Life and Death

A few days later, things had calmed down a little. Megan and Ryan had both spoken to the police and Ryan got his phone back, much to his surprise. It seemed that by the time the police got to the gatehouse, Joe had gone, but later on he walked into a police station and gave himself up for questioning. Megan was secretly pleased that Joe had not made the situation worse for Sarah and Alice.

Paul said very little to Megan about Joe over the next few weeks and she didn't ask him anything. She didn't want to spoil things for him. He seemed to be calmer than she had ever known him. He even kept his promise to write to Irene and a few days later they spoke on the phone for a very long time. Megan had no idea what they had talked about, but she was astounded when her dad told her he had accepted an invitation to visit Irene in the next few weeks.

On the day that Megan called to tell Ryan the news about her dad and Irene, it had been snowing all morning, even though it was early March. Megan decided to wear the new coat she'd bought when she went shopping with Kirsty. She thought she looked so grown up in it, but Ryan didn't seem to notice. He was looking very pleased with himself.

'We're moving into part of our new house next month,' he

announced. 'We can only live in a couple of rooms, but it will be better than staying cooped up here with my grandad.'

Megan tried to sound pleased for Ryan, but she had come to rely on his company in her search for the truth and she knew she would miss him.

'Will you stay on at Oakton school?' asked Megan.

'Definitely,' said Ryan. 'It's OK there. It's not like it used to be. It's a really good school now.'

Megan was surprised. 'Is it?'

'Yeah. You should tell your dad. He might change his mind and let you go there, if that's what you want.'

'I don't want to move schools any more,' said Megan. 'I've made friends with a girl called Rosa. She's my best friend now. It's amazing how we like the same things…'

Ryan got up and looked out of the window. He didn't seem interested in Megan's school friends. 'It's stopped snowing,' he said. 'Shall we go to Irene's? I want to find out if Tom's come back. We'll leave Skippy here.'

Megan had almost forgotten about the wild cats. If Ryan hadn't seen the blood on the snow and found the wild cat in the watchtower, she would never have started the long journey to find out the truth about her mother.

As they walked along the woodland path, Megan noticed how beautiful everything looked, covered in the light snow. 'It's just like the day you took me to see Zoe,' said Megan. 'Except there are snowdrops and crocuses under the snow now.'

'She was a pretty scary cat, wasn't she?' said Ryan. 'I'd never seen anything so wild and fierce.'

'Come on,' said Megan, 'let's go and have a look at the watchtower again.'

As they walked up the crooked path behind the bench, signs of the blackening fire peeped out from under a faint carpet of fine snow. 'It's like a different world up here now,' said Megan.

They stared into the tower. 'A lot's happened since we were last here, hasn't it?' said Ryan. Megan nodded.

'I was wrong about Kirsty, wasn't I?' he said suddenly. 'She's always so cheerful. I can't believe she's been burnt in a fire and lost one of the dogs like that.'

'She runs to raise money for the hospital burns unit,' said Megan. 'That's where they treated her hands.'

'I got her completely wrong didn't I?' admitted Ryan.

'You can't always tell what people have been through,' replied Megan wisely.

Ryan looked visibly upset. 'What's wrong?' asked Megan.

'My step-mum is always so cheerful. It gets to me sometimes, but she was ill last year and she nearly died,' he said softly.

'Is that why your dad wants to build her a new house?' asked Megan.

'Yes,' said Ryan. 'I didn't want to move from London. I was angry with everyone, but now I feel awful. At least I've got both parents still alive and I've even got a step-mum.'

'You never talk about your real mum,' said Megan. 'When will you see her again?'

'She works for a company in London,' said Ryan. 'Last year the company sent her to America and I thought she wasn't ever coming back, but now it looks like she is.'

'When will you see her then?' asked Megan again.

'I'm going to stay with her in the summer holidays,' said Ryan excitedly. 'She still has her flat. You can see right across London from the balcony.'

'Good,' said Megan. 'I'm glad.'

They turned and walked away down the path, each absorbed in their own thoughts, until they reached the gatehouses. Irene's car was outside, but when they knocked on her door there was no answer. 'Maybe she's in the garden,' said Megan. 'Let's go round the back.'

Irene heard them coming and opened the gate to let them in. Her face looked red and puffy, as if she'd been crying.

'Is something wrong Irene?' asked Megan.

'I found Tom this morning in his pen,' she said tearfully. 'He looked so peaceful. I thought he was asleep but, when I looked closer, I could see he'd been injured and all the life had gone from him.'

It was then that Megan noticed the white blanket covering something on the floor of one of the pens. The edges of the white blanket were tinged with red blood. Megan didn't know what to say. 'I'm so sorry,' she whispered.

'He came back here to die,' said Irene.

'Did something attack him?' asked Ryan.

'Yes, but I'm not sure what,' said Irene. 'It could have been anything. He was an old cat and not as strong as he used to be.'

There was a long pause, as they both tried to take in the information.

'His time had come,' said Irene as she brushed away a tear. 'That's just how it is.'

Megan looked again at the blanket. Although she didn't blame the wild cat for running in front of her mother's car, it's death felt like some kind of ending to her search for the truth.

'I'm going to bury him over there,' said Irene, pointing to a small grassy area beside the pens. 'I thought I might plant a small tree next to his grave.'

'That would be nice,' said Megan.

'We can help bury him if you like,' offered Ryan.

'Thanks,' replied Irene, 'but it's something I'd like to do on my own. We go back a long way, Tom and I, and it will be the last thing I ever do for him.'

'Anyway,' she said, suddenly brightening up, 'I'm glad

you're here, because I've got something really good to show you.'

They followed Irene towards the pen near the shed, where Zoe was sprawled out on some bedding. The cat growled as they approached, but she didn't move.

'Come nearer,' said Irene speaking softly. 'Look closer. Tell me what you can see.'

Megan peered into the pen. Underneath Zoe, she could just see a tiny tail. It was tawny in colour with thin stripes. Then she saw another tail and something else moved into the light. Ryan gasped as two kittens emerged, making tiny sounds with their bright red mouths and wobbling about. 'So that's why her stomach was swollen,' said Megan.

Irene looked pleased. 'By the look of them, I think Tom was their father,' she said proudly.

'So that makes them pure wild cats,' said Ryan.

'Mike would be so proud to have bred these wild cats,' said Irene, 'but I've decided to take them back to Scotland. To the Highlands where they belong.'

Ryan was shocked. 'Why?'

'A woman from the newspaper phoned me yesterday,' said Irene angrily. 'An anonymous caller told her they'd seen two large animal pens in my garden and she accused me of putting lives at risk by keeping big cats.'

'I hope you told her to get lost,' said Ryan.

'She threatened to call the police, if I didn't give her the full story,' said Irene.

'But it's not true that you're keeping big cats,' said Ryan indignantly. 'You said yourself that they're wild cats, not big cats. Did you tell the journalist that?'

'Yes, but she said they were still dangerous,' replied Irene.

Ryan was becoming more and more angry. 'But they're not dangerous. They won't attack for no reason and they wouldn't kill anyone even if they did.'

Irene sighed. 'I can't say for certain that Zoe wouldn't attack a dog or even livestock,' she said. 'After all, they are killers by instinct, but I won't have Zoe hunted down.' She paused reflectively. 'It'll be lonely for her now anyway. Now she's lost her mate.'

'Will you just release them, when you get to the Highlands?' asked Megan.

Irene smiled. 'No. I've found a zoo park there. They'll integrate Zoe back into the wild gradually, but her kittens will be truly wild.'

'I'm glad they're going to be free,' said Megan.

As they went out of the gate, Irene called them back. 'Just a minute Megan. I've got something for you. I almost forgot.' She disappeared into the house and when she came back she was carrying the little basket of knitted cats. She handed the basket to Megan. 'This belongs to you,' she said. 'It was your seventh birthday present. You left it behind.'

Megan took it from her with great care. 'Thank you,' she whispered.

'I knitted the little cats myself,' said Irene.

'They're lovely,' said Megan. Then she reached out her arms and gave Irene a big hug.

By the time Megan got home, she had made a decision about where to put the basket of cats. She would put it on her shelf, next to the birthday card that her mum and dad sent her on her seventh birthday.

Paul was waiting for Megan when she got home. She was worried he might get upset, when he saw the basket of cats, but he just smiled.

'Sit down Megan,' he said gently. 'I have something for you.'

She noticed there was a letter in his hand and she hoped it

wasn't bad news. Paul unfolded the handwritten letter and took out a small card. 'This is for you,' he said.

The card was hand-made. It was covered in pink shiny stars. Inside the card was a photograph of a little girl with red curly hair, just like Megan's. She knew who it was from, even before she read the childish writing inside:

Deer Megan
Plees can you cum and play with me
Love from cusin Alice xxx

She looked at her dad in amazement.

'I wrote to Sarah,' said Paul, 'and she's written back. This card was inside her letter. I've been talking to Kirsty and she convinced me it was the right thing to do. Everyone says Sarah's a good person and I think it's about time you met your cousin.'

'She looks just like me,' said Megan.

'And she looks just like Maggie too,' said Paul smiling.

'By the way,' he added, 'I'm not sure how I feel about you seeing Joe, but Andy told me some news about him today.'

'What sort of news?' asked Megan anxiously.

'It seems we've misjudged him,' said Paul. 'It was the two youths working at Ray's carwash who carried out all the burglaries. When they thought the police might search their flat, they hid a bag of stolen goods in an old watchtower in the woods. But the police found it and managed to trace it back to them. It's amazing what the police can do these days.'

'I don't understand,' said Megan. 'You caught Joe trying to steal things from Bill's shed.'

'Well, that's where we all jumped to the wrong conclusions,' said Paul. 'He was in the shed, but he wasn't trying to steal anything.'

Megan looked confused. 'What was he doing in the shed then?' she asked.

'It's a bit complicated,' said Paul, 'but as far as I can make out, the loud noise you heard that night was the two youths from the carwash at Ray's garage, breaking the lock on Bill's shed. We think they were after the car parts.'

'So, was it their torches that I saw?' asked Megan.

'It was,' said Paul.

'But I still don't get it,' said Megan. 'How come Joe was coming out of the shed when you got there and where were the two youths?'

Paul tried to explain as best he could. 'Joe was on one of his night-time runs that evening. He was running along the back lane, behind our houses, when he heard a loud bang and went to investigate. When he realised that someone had broken into Bill's shed, he went in to confront them. The two youths put up a fight, but when Joe collapsed after banging his head, they got scared and ran off empty-handed.'

'All this must have happened when I was upstairs trying to wake you up,' said Megan.

'That's right,' said Paul. 'By the time I got there, the youths had gone and all I saw was Joe staggering out of the shed. I thought he was drunk, but he was still dazed from his fall.'

'Why didn't he just tell you what had happened?' asked Megan.

Paul sighed. 'He didn't really get much chance, did he? It all happened so quickly. When I saw it was Joe, I was so angry that I just went for him. Then Bill threatened him with the gun and he ran off.'

'Maybe he was confused after his fall,' suggested Megan.

'Maybe,' said Paul. 'But Andy thinks the sight of Bill's gun might have reminded him of bad times in the army. Maybe that's why he just pushed Bill away and ran off without saying anything.'

Megan looked relieved. 'So, Joe isn't a burglar after all.'

'It doesn't look like it.' said Paul.

Megan thought for a moment. 'I think I understand what happened that night now Dad,' she said, 'but why did Joe hide in the empty gatehouse? Why did he hide at all, if he wasn't guilty?'

Paul shrugged his shoulders. 'I'm not sure,' he said, 'but according to Bill he often camped out in the woods when things got too much for him. Maybe he was so shaken up after the incident with the gun that he needed to be alone to think it all through.'

'Well whatever the reason, I'm glad he's innocent,' said Megan. 'I don't think he's a bad person really.'

Paul shook his head. 'He may not be a bad person Megan, but he needs some help with his anger, that's for sure.' Megan didn't say anything, but she suddenly saw a similarity between Joe and her dad and she hoped they would both find peace someday.

'Night Dad,' said Megan that evening, as she headed up the stairs.

'Wait a minute,' said Paul. 'I've been up in the loft today and I've got something for you.' He handed her a large photograph in a silver frame. It was a photo of her mother, taken when she won a local art competition.

'It was taken just before she died,' said Paul. 'Her painting won first prize.'

Megan took a closer look at the photo. Her mum was standing proudly beside a painting of a little girl with red curly hair. 'Is that me?' she said slowly.

Paul nodded. 'I thought you might like to keep it in your room.'

Megan reached out for her dad's hand. It was shaking. 'Thanks Dad,' she whispered. 'Do we still have the painting?'

'It's probably in the loft with all the others she painted,' said Paul.

'Maybe we'll look at them together some time?' said Megan hopefully.

'Yes,' said Paul, 'but not just yet.'

'I understand,' said Megan and she hugged him tight, just like she used to when she was a little girl.

That night Megan began to think about everything that had happened since she set off to stalk Ryan on that cold February night. It was the end of her search for the truth, but now there were lots of beginnings to look forward to. Her dad was improving, she had got to know Ryan, Irene and Kirsty and she was much happier at school, now Rosa was her best friend. Then there was her newly found uncle Joe and her little cousin Alice.

She took another look at the photo of her mother holding the painting. 'I think I know what happened now, Mum,' she whispered, as she placed the photo on her shelf. 'But it's taken me a long time to find out.'

She opened a drawer in her bedside table and took out a large notebook. It had a red velvet cover with tiny gold hearts along the spine. It was the one she was saving for something special. 'You know what I'm going to do now, Mum?' she said. 'I'm going to write everything down in a story, so if I have any children of my own, they will know how I discovered the truth about their grandmother.' She paused to think for a moment. 'I'm going to call my story *Red Snow*,' she said, 'because everything started to change after Ryan saw Zoe's red blood on the snow. She took a pen from the drawer and began to write:

RED SNOW
Chapter One: The Stalker
Stalking the boy next door in the middle of the night was not one of my most sensible decisions, but, in the end, it turned out to be one of my best...